Sarah with love from Leonard
Christmas 1981

Winter's Tales 27

Winter's Tales 27

Edited by
Edward Leeson

ISBN 0 333 310721

First published 1981 by
Macmillan London Limited
London and Basingstoke

Associated companies in Auckland, Dallas,
Delhi, Dublin, Hong Kong, Johannesburg,
Lagos, Manzini, Melbourne, Nairobi,
New York, Singapore, Tokyo, Washington
and Zaria

Phototypeset in Linotron 202 Palatino by
Western Printing Services Ltd. Bristol
Printed in Great Britain

Contents

Acknowledgements

The stories are copyright respectively:

© 1981 Philip Oakes
© 1981 V. S. Pritchett
© 1981 Celia Dale
© 1981 Harold Acton
© 1981 Terence Wheeler
© 1981 Giles Gordon
© 1981 Brunner Fact & Fiction
© 1981 Murray Bail
© 1981 Graham Swift
© 1981 M. John Harrison
© 1981 Fay Weldon
© 1980 Leslie Thomas

Leslie Thomas's 'Christmas with a Stranger' was first published in *The New Standard*, 24 December 1980.

Editor's Note

Winter's Tales 27 offers the blend of new writers and old masters which has been characteristic of *Winter's Tales* from the very beginning more than a quarter of a century ago, and readers will notice several unfamiliar names as well as some well-known ones.

The twelve stories amply demonstrate, by their variety of subject and style, the versatility of the short-story form. In this connection I might mention Harold Acton's study of Latin passion, which is itself part of a series of Florentine portraits to be published soon, M. John Harrison's elusive and thought-provoking 'Egnaro', and Leslie Thomas's hilarious but touching fairy-tale with which the volume ends; while John Brunner, already well known to science-fiction enthusiasts, has contributed a macabre and surprising tale full of strange, twists and turns.

Winter's Tales 27 was prepared at a time when, once again, the immediate prospects for publishing, and for the writer of fiction, appeared bleak. Nevertheless, in spite of such dire forecasts, devotion to the short story remains undiminished, and *Winter's Tales* continues to provide a forum.

EDWARD LEESON

Letting the Birds Go Free

Philip Oakes

'Hit him again,' said my father, so I hit the stranger in the face and stood over him as he fell heavily into the grass, powdery with small white seeds. He made no attempt to get up, but lay on his back, staring into our faces and licking his lips. A few seeds clung to his hair and stuck in the trickle of blood that oozed from one nostril.

'Get up,' said my father, but the stranger shook his head.

'Stay there, then,' said my father and, taking out his tobacco-pouch, he rolled a cigarette while he made up his mind what to do next.

There was not much we could do until the stranger decided to co-operate. There is a limit to the number of times you can knock a man down. He had been knocked down twice already, and if we wanted him off our land we had to carry him. He lay there and watched us.

It was a Friday morning. Every day that week someone had stolen eggs from the hen-run. It sounds a trivial matter, but it was important to my father. What money was his he had earned by hard work, and the idea of a thief getting something for nothing exasperated him. He was not an unreasonable man, but he kept a close watch on his returns. A cow whose milk yield was failing was sold without hesitation and a horse had to earn its keep or make the long trip to the knacker's yard. I once saw my father shoot a yard dog because it failed to give the alarm when a set of harness was stolen from the stable.

When the egg takings fell below average he at first blamed the hens and stared resentfully at the flock that pecked and squabbled about his feet as if to divine which bird to single out for punishment. Then we found that a window in one of the huts had been forced open and the next day we set out to catch the thief.

It was early June and already warm at five o'clock. When we left home there was no one near the hen-run. We squatted down by the wall and waited. The grass in the bottom meadow looked like silk, green one minute and silver the next as the wind pressed it gently over. A pair of swallows twittered liquidly under the roof of the Dutch barn, and suddenly one of them flew out in a long ascending curve that was broken as the bird tumbled aside to catch a fly. We sat there for half an hour while the dew dried, and then I saw a man climbing the wall on the opposite side of the field. We did not move but watched him cross the spoiled grass of the hen-run, raise the window and squeeze through. He was very slight to be able to do so. My father sat still, resting back on his heels, a blue tattooed flag waving steadily over the muscles of his forearm. He waited for another minute, then stood up and walked briskly towards the hut.

A few moments later the stranger climbed out of the window. He saw us before he touched the ground and for a count of three remained poised awkwardly, his feet pointed earthwards. Then he let himself down and looked at us each in turn. He was twenty or so, a small fair man wearing a check shirt and a pair of oily blue jeans. The sleeves of his shirt were buttoned down, and he wore town shoes. He did not try to run away but stood waiting, an egg in each hand. My father looked at the eggs and turned to me.

'Hit him,' he said.

I cuffed the man on the side of the head and he fell down. The eggs bounced on the grass and one of them broke. My father picked up the egg that was unbroken and stroked the smooth brown shell with his thumb. 'Lift him,' he said. I caught hold of the stranger's shirt and hauled him to his feet. 'Hit him again,' said my father, and I did as I was told.

He lay in the grass and looked at us.

'This is my land,' said my father. 'These are my hens and these are my eggs. You're a thief.'

The stranger did not reply but lay where he was, tasting the blood that slowly covered his lip.

'Can you pay for them?' asked my father, and the man shook his head.

'Can you work?' asked my father, and the stranger nodded.

'Anything to do with engines,' he said. He was not from our part of the world. He had a sharp town accent.

My father studied the burning end of his cigarette. 'Do you know anything about tractors?'

'I know about tractors.'

It was a statement made without asperity, but the implication was obvious. Any fool knew about tractors. He made no move to get up but brushed a grass seed from the corner of his eye and allowed the interview to proceed.

'Reapers? Binders?'

'I know about them, too.'

My knuckles were bleeding from where I had cut them on his teeth. A milk-lorry unloaded churns a mile up the road and they clattered as they hit the ground.

My father plucked a scrap of paper from his lip. 'Are you working?'

The stranger shook his head and smiled. I had chipped one of his teeth.

'Do you want a job?'

'With engines?'

My father nodded briefly. The man on the ground considered the proposition.

'I don't mind,' he said.

'Help him up,' said my father, and I gave the man my hand. He was no weight at all. He dusted himself down and blew his nose with his fingers. My father finished his cigarette and stood waiting. 'What's your name?' he asked.

'Harry Fisher,' said the stranger.

'My name's Arthur King and this is my son Eddie,' said my father. 'When I'm not here you'll take orders from him.'

'I don't take orders from anyone,' said Harry Fisher mildly. 'I'm not that sort of chap.'

'Instructions, then. He'll tell you what needs to be done.'

'Everyone's got to learn, but I don't take orders,' he said. He spoke as though he had made the point many times before and had found it necessary to do so. He expected opposition.

We walked to the road in single file along the ditch beside the wall. My father led the way, and Harry Fisher followed him. He had long fair hair the colour of dried grass that bounced lightly on his head. His hands were deep in his pockets and he dragged his feet. My father held the gate open and closed it when we had passed through. 'Always close gates,' he said. 'Cattle stray.'

'They keep nothing out,' said Harry.

'There's not many want to get in,' said my father.

Up at the house he took Harry into the kitchen and showed him where he could wash; then he joined me in the yard.

'Well, what do you think?' he asked.

'He's built like a girl.'

'You don't need muscles to turn a spanner,' said my father. 'Anyroad, he'll fatten up.'

'On our food,' I said.

My father scratched his nose where the dead skin was peeling off. 'He'll earn his keep, I reckon.'

My father was a short man, brown-skinned and almost bald. He wore a flannel shirt fastened at the neck by a brass stud, a black waistcoat over leather braces, and twill working-trousers. His face was thin and deeply lined, his eyes a startling blue. He was honest, industrious, jealous and occasionally violent. Above all, though, my father was a passionate man. He concealed his passion by a ceaseless preoccupation with work that was in itself a passion of another kind. He had loved my mother deeply, but on the day of her funeral he left the church and came home alone to do the milking. When he was angry his anger remained with him like a stone in the hand until he could expel it forcibly. He was careful never to waste it by attempting

something that was beyond his powers. The failure to suc-
ceed would only have angered him further. It was for this
reason that he had not hit Harry Fisher himself. He was
over sixty and I was half his age. Therefore, he reasoned, I
was better suited to the job in hand, and through me he had
spent his rage.

In his way he was also capable of great gentleness. I once
saw him set a cat's broken leg, encasing it in a cast he made
from pulped newspapers and soap. She had kittens a week
later, holding the cast stiffly to one side like a drumstick
while the kittens slid out in small steaming parcels. She was
a good ratter, said my father, so she was worth looking
after. It was true, of course, but he offered the explanation as
he would an apology. He would have hated to have been
thought soft.

At the same time, he never attempted to excuse his abid-
ing interest in birds, although he might have regarded it as a
weakness in another man. He showed me my first kestrel's
nest at the top of a Douglas fir and taught me how to find the
grass-lined scrapes of peewits in the furrows of a ploughed
field. The trick, he said, was to plant a stick in the middle of
the field and walk towards it in ever-diminishing circles
until you had covered the whole area. He allowed me to
take one egg from each nest and sat with me at the kitchen
table while I turned them this way and that, tracing the
blotches and the hieroglyphs that inscribed the olive shells
like secret writing.

That spring he had rescued a family of young bullfinches
which had been washed out of their nest in a waste-pipe by
heavy rain. For weeks he fed them a mixture of water-
softened bread and mealworms, transferring them when
they were ready to fly into a large triple cage shaped like an
Indian temple which had once housed my mother's pet
parrot. It had been an evil-tempered bird, and only she had
loved it; but when it died we gave it a proper funeral and its
grave in the garden was still marked with a stone. I much
preferred the finches. There were three cocks and a hen, my
father's favourite. She was quite tame, and in the evenings

he would let her out to follow a trail of seed up his arm and across his shoulders. As he ate his supper she perched on the neckband of his shirt, plucking at the long hairs on his neck, twisting and braiding them as if she were preparing a nest. She took food from my father's mouth and they talked to each other in whistles and sweet sibilants. Soon, said my father, he would teach her to sing a simple tune.

'We'll be busy the next few weeks,' he reminded me. 'We always reckon to take on another man part-time in the summer. It's as well to have one on tap.'

We went into the kitchen where Harry was combing his hair in front of the shaving-mirror. It was a small square of chipped glass, hung too low for comfort, and he had to bend his knees to see his reflection. He had washed the blood from his face and he looked better. His upper lip was swollen.

'Are you done?' asked my father.

Harry slid the comb into his hip pocket. 'I'm done,' he said.

'You'd best have some breakfast with us,' said my father. 'Go on through.'

He went into the living-room where the finches flirted backwards and forwards behind their bars and my sister Grace was laying the table. My father had made it a rule that no meals should be eaten in the kitchen. 'Farmhands eat in muck and mud, but farmers eat in comfort,' he maintained. He insisted that the cloth should be clean and the meal properly served. Hurried meals, poorly presented, implied carelessness and bad husbandry. He had a good appetite and enjoyed good food. He sat down and turned to Harry. 'How many eggs can you eat?'

'One,' said Harry.

'Bring him two,' said my father.

Grace paused at the door. 'Do you like your bacon crisp or not?'

'It doesn't matter,' said Harry. He hesitated. 'Crisp.'

Grace went out, closing the door behind her. She was nineteen that summer, taller than my father and broad, with breasts that moved softly beneath her overall. She had my mother's face, oval and fair-skinned, with straight black hair and eyebrows. She had brown eyes and fat white arms that burned in the sun.

The nearest farm was a mile up the road, and Grace had few women friends. She went to school in the mill town at the other end of the valley until she was sixteen, when my father decided that she was old enough to take charge of the housekeeping. He paid her a small wage, and Grace was not displeased. It did not occur to her to ask for anything more. Once a week she went to the cinema, catching the midday bus outside the gate and returning home on the eleven o'clock bus at night. A circulating-library van called at the house on Tuesdays and Fridays, its windows plastered with dust-jackets from Western novels and romances, and Grace chose her book by the picture on the cover.

She was not a great reader, but she preferred the printed page to television. Sometimes I caught her watching the commercials in which girls demonstrated lipstick, pouting gigantically from the small screen, their black-fringed eyes staring boldly into our living-room. They made her uncomfortable. So did the advertisements for holidays abroad in which lithe young couples, glinting with gold, drank apéritifs by swimming-pools or walked hand in hand through a foaming carpet of surf.

'Do you fancy that?' I asked her once.

'Fat chance,' she said.

'Why not? We could afford it.'

'Who would I go with? There's no one round here wants to go to those places.'

'You could go with me. I'd keep out of the way and let you find a millionaire.'

She shook her head. 'I'd feel daft. What would I say to folks?'

'The same as you'd say to anyone else.'

'Small talk, you mean. Something about the price of eggs. Or swine fever. Clever stuff like that?'

'You know what I mean,' I said. 'You just need to be natural.'

'Un-natural, more like.' She nodded towards the set. 'It's the only way I'd manage with folk like that.'

Our conversations were rarely so intimate. We accepted each other as members of the same household. At Christmas we bought each other presents, and our disagreements arose from the small jealousies between brother and sister. Love had never brought us so close together.

She sang in the kitchen while she cooked breakfast. My father poured out three cups of tea and handed one to Harry.

'I'll give you twenty quid and your keep.'

'A week?'

My father nodded.

'You'll have the best of everything while you're here. You needn't spend a penny.'

'There's not many pennies to spend,' said Harry amiably. 'What did you pay your last man?'

My father set down his cup.

'That's got nothing to do with it. He wasn't living in.'

'Twenty-five,' suggested Harry. 'It's less than the going rate.'

They looked at each other across the table, and unexpectedly my father smiled. 'We'll see,' he said. 'You'll get what you're worth.'

Harry Fisher had not been boasting when he said that he knew about engines. He stripped and reassembled the tractor and presented my father with a list of new parts that were needed. When he questioned one or two items Harry shrugged his shoulders. 'You're saving the mechanic's wage,' he said.

He moved into my room on the north side of the house over the kitchen, and I offered him a couple of working-shirts and a pair of pyjamas that I had outgrown. 'I'll borrow them,' he said. 'Till I buy my own.'

At that time we were taking our eggs to town twice a week and selling them to a stall-holder in the market. Our main business, though, was breeding birds for the table. They were a cross between game fowl and Rhode Island Reds, and each month we despatched a thousand or more to hotels and restaurants all over the country. We killed and dressed them on the farm. Each bird had its neck wrung – it was neater than a knife, said my father – then it was plucked mechanically, gutted and parcelled in plastic. We sent them off in cardboard coffins from the local station. We also kept a house cow and grew enough wheat and vegetables for our own needs. The eggs paid Grace's wage and supplied her with pocket money, too. It was half an hour's drive each way with a wait in the market while the business was transacted. Grace could not drive the van, so that either my father or myself had to do it. We grudged the time spent, and after a week Harry was given the job.

He waited in the kitchen while Grace packed the eggs in their trays. He did not offer to help, but whistled softly and cleaned his nails with a matchstick.

'You can start putting them in the van,' said Grace.

Harry looked up, nodded and continued to clean his nails.

'In a minute.'

'You've not got all day,' she said.

Harry looked at her curiously for a second and then took the eggs out to the van. She watched him go, swaggering a little with the trays held in front of him, treading carefully up the path to the road.

It was a still, bright morning with small clouds edging imperceptibly across the wide sky. Harry opened the door of the van and slid the trays in the back. It tilted with his weight and trembled as he slammed the door. It was an old Transit, blue where the paint remained and red with rust where it had flaked off. He re-entered the kitchen and waited until Grace filled the last of the trays.

'You can go now,' she said, scrubbing her hands with the towel. 'There's nothing to hang about for.'

Harry grinned and went without a word. The van shook as he started the engine and stood quivering like a tired horse while he wound down the window. He leaned out and waved to Grace and then drove away.

'Cheek,' she said. 'Who does he think he's waving at?' She stamped upstairs and I heard her slapping the beds in our room over the kitchen.

Harry was not home by lunch-time, and I was mending a wall in the top meadow when I heard the van on the road below. It was going fast and swerving senselessly from side to side. It shot past the gate of the farm, stopped suddenly, reversed and stopped again. Harry got out and fell face downwards on the road. The engine was still running.

I saw my father watching from the top of a ladder against the silo he was building. He pulled down the peak of his cap and steadily climbed down the ladder. Grace came out of the house and ran towards the van. She and my father met over Harry's body. I fitted a small stone into place and went to join them.

'He's had a skinful,' said my father.

I bent over and smelled the beer on Harry's breath. 'He did well to get back,' I said. 'It's a wonder he wasn't picked up.'

My father turned back to the van and switched off the engine. He reached into the van and then slammed the door shut. 'He's had a good day's shopping,' he said, displaying two shirts still folded in their cellophane jackets and a small parcel wrapped in brown paper.

I lifted Harry to his feet and half-carried him into the house. My father followed us into the kitchen and dropped the packages on to the table. 'I'll see him when he's sober,' he said. 'You'd best let him sleep it off.'

Harry half-opened his eyes and muttered something unintelligible. My father made a gesture of disgust and walked angrily back towards the road.

'Drink,' said Harry.

I raised his head. 'What happened to you?'

'Drink,' he said again.

'As though he'd not had enough,' said Grace. She filled a

cup with water and gave it to him. 'He's disgusting,' she said.

Harry stroked her wrist. 'Brought you a present,' he said. He tilted the cup to his mouth and slopped water over his shirt and thighs. 'Present,' he said, pointing to the table. 'There.'

I picked up the small parcel wrapped in brown paper and gave it to Grace.

'Open it,' said Harry.

She still hesitated.

'Go on,' he said.

She broke the string and uncovered a small white box. Harry leaned forward in his chair and almost slipped to the floor.

'Go on,' he said. 'Open it.'

Grace held the box to her body and removed the lid. She looked inside and then quickly put it on the table. The box contained a bottle of scent shaped like a pyramid. There was more glass and stopper than there was liquid inside.

'For you to wear,' said Harry seriously. 'I feel bad.'

Grace walked out into the yard, leaving the scent on the table, and I helped Harry to the sink. He was violently sick. I turned on the tap and let the water run. He shivered and ducked his head under the tap, massaging his scalp with slow fingers. 'Oh, Jesus,' he said.

The water darkened his hair, and his fingers raked it into spikes. He breathed laboriously in self-pity. I took his arm. 'Better get some fresh air.'

He jerked his face upwards. 'There's nothing but bloody fresh air here.'

He followed me up the path, over the road and across the fields to the top meadow, tripping over tussocks of grass and swearing each time he did so. His shirt front was saturated, and in the sunlight his hair began to steam gently. By the time we had reached the wall he was out of breath. He sat down untidily and blew his nose.

I left him sitting there and went on mending the wall. He did not speak for some time, but I felt him watching me. Finally: 'Is the van all right?'

'It's all right.'

'I'd better see,' he said. 'What did Grace say?'

'Nothing much,' I said. 'You'd best have a word with my father.'

He chewed a stem of grass and spat it out as though he had discovered suddenly that he disliked the taste and rose awkwardly to his feet. 'All right,' he said. He paused for a moment. 'I had a few drinks. Out of my wages.'

'Out of the egg money.'

'I had my wages coming,' he said. 'I only spent what was mine.'

'Tell that to the old man.'

'I will,' he said shortly. 'I'll tell him now.' He set off towards the road and then turned round. 'You can have your shirts back. I bought some.' He went on again, almost running as he neared the bottom of the meadow.

Later that afternoon I met my father in the milking-shed. 'Did you see Harry?' I asked him. He nodded non-committally and pressed his head against the cow's brown flank. With only one beast, we did the milking by hand. Thin jets of milk drummed on the bottom of the pail and erupted briefly in a froth of bubbles.

'What's happening?' I persisted.

'Nothing,' said my father. 'What he spent was his own.' He had made up his mind and there was no more to be said. The cow shifted contrarily, and he butted his head against the side. 'Keep still,' he said.

The box containing the scent was no longer on the table when I entered the kitchen. Harry was adding up a column of figures with a bundle of notes and a few coins in front of him. He was wearing a clean shirt. Grace prepared tea, moving noisily about the stove. Her hair was freshly combed and she wore a tight red jumper beneath her over-all. She was also wearing the scent. I smelled it as she leaned over Harry to get a spoon from the drawer of the table and her bare arm brushed the side of his face. He shied away in confusion.

'I'm sorry,' said Grace, still bending over him.

Harry looked rigidly at the table, aware of the warmth of her breasts so close to him. 'You made me jump,' he said, not daring to move until she drew back. 'I was doing my sums.'

They were both conscious of a new intimacy, desirous and yet afraid of it. Afraid, too, that others could see it also.

In the night I woke to see him standing by the window, his face striped by moonlight. I turned over restlessly.

'Can't sleep,' he said. 'It's like day out here.'

The yard, the road, the meadow and the moor were bleached by the moon. It was very quiet and there was no wind.

'Does the old man like me?' asked Harry.

'He must do,' I said.

He sat down so that his face was in shadow. 'I meant to push off this morning. I had the van and I had the money. I could have got clear away. You know nothing about me. You'd never have seen me again.' He returned to the window so that his face was lit by the cold radiance. 'I told the old man, and what d'you think he said?' He threw out his hands violently.

'He said it would have been a bad bargain but he knew I wouldn't take off like that.' Harry crossed the floor in two anguished steps and stood by my bed. 'How did he know that?' he demanded. 'I didn't know myself. I meant to push off. None of you knows me. You don't know what I might do.'

'I don't know anything,' I said. 'I want to get back to sleep.'

He plucked at my blankets. 'How d'you think I happened to turn up here?'

'You got lost.'

'I was on the run,' he said. 'My regiment's in Ulster. We've done one stretch already, and they were sending us back for a second tour. I couldn't face it.' He sat down on my bed and rested his chin in his hands. 'You don't know what it's like,' he said.

'I've seen it on the telly.'

'It's worse than that. They don't show you half. A mate of mine was killed. They booby-trapped the car. They blew his guts out.'

'That's terrible,' I said.

'They don't want us there. We ought to sod off. It's not our country. I don't want to shoot anyone.'

'Does Grace know about this?' I asked.

'She knows.'

'Are you going to tell the old man?'

He glared up at the ceiling. 'Christ only knows. What would he do about it?'

'You'll have to ask him,' I said. 'I won't say anything. It's not up to me.'

He got back into bed and lay without speaking for several seconds. The moonlight poured through the window and I turned my back on it. The bedsprings creaked loudly as though Harry had raised himself on one elbow to continue the conversation. There was an interval and then he lay down again. 'Good-night,' he said. We both went to sleep.

It was in August that the police called. Harry had gone to town to collect the parts for the tractor, and my father and I were laying a path from the kitchen door to the road. We saw the police car pass the bottom meadow where the grass was thick and ready for a second cut, then drive on towards us. When it stopped the driver remained at the wheel and the other man got out of the car and walked carefully up the unmade path. He had a thin red face and fair, almost invisible eyebrows. When he took off his cap to wipe his forehead I saw that the rim had bitten into the skin like a rabbit-snare. His name was George Marsden and we had been in the same class at school.

He nodded pleasantly and loosened his tie. 'Morning, Arthur. Eddie.' We nodded back. 'Nice crop,' he said, indicating the bottom meadow.

'If it stays fine,' said my father. 'A bit more sun and we'll do nicely.'

'It doesn't look like rain,' said George Marsden. 'I reckon it'll hold out for you.'

'On your way somewhere?' asked my father.

'Here,' said George. 'You've got a new chap working for you.'

My father unbuttoned his tobacco-pouch. 'That's right.'

'Can I have a word with him?'

'He's out,' I said. 'Is there anything we can do?'

'What's his name?' asked George. 'Where does he come from?'

My father licked the gummed edge of his cigarette-paper and rolled it between his fingers. 'His name's Harry Fisher and he lives here.'

'Where does he come from?' asked George officially.

'You'd best ask Harry,' said my father. 'I'll tell him you want to see him.'

'Mind if I wait?' asked George.

'He'll be a good while,' said my father. 'He's got the van. I'll tell him to look in when he gets back.'

George thrust his face forward so that another half-inch of his neck protruded from his shirt collar. 'You think he'll come when he knows I want to see him?'

'I'll tell him,' said my father neutrally.

'Look,' said George. 'At the station they think he's an army deserter. They think he's the chap that broke into the school and the grocer's. That's why I want to see him.'

'I'll tell him,' said my father.

'He'll go the other way. I'd better wait,' said George. He looked for a place to sit down and then, after a few minutes' consideration, approached us again. 'Will you see that he comes to the station, Arthur?' he asked more quietly.

'I've already told you what I'll do,' said my father.

George Marsden looked at me.

'He might not be the man,' I said.

George put on his cap. 'I've another call to make, but I'll be back,' he said. 'If he's here before then, make him wait.'

He walked stiffly away.

'Make him?' said my father. 'Harry wouldn't like that.'

We went into the house. In the living-room the garden door was open and, as we entered, a bullfinch flew from the top of the cage and out into the raspberry-canes. The cage was still secure and there were still four birds inside it.

'What's going on now?' I said.

My father pointed to the little hen. She was dashing herself against the bars and falling back on to the floor of the cage. Her beak gaped and her feathers were ruffled. 'She's had a visitor,' he said. 'There's been a cock come courting.'

I went to close the garden door, but he motioned me to leave it open.

'Is it right what he said about Harry?'

'Right enough,' I said. 'They were sending him back to Ireland for a second time. He couldn't stand that.'

'Does Grace know?'

'Harry told her,' I said. 'I reckon he'd have told you by and by.'

He nodded slowly. 'I reckon he would.'

'We can't turn him in,' I said. 'We can't let George have him.'

'I never said we should,' said my father. 'We'd best let him know what's happening. Grace can catch him at the corner. There's some wages owing him. He'll be needing money if he's to stay loose.'

'And his clothes,' I said. 'She'd better pack a case.'

My father snapped open the front of his pocket watch. 'If he catches the twelve o'clock, he'll be in Manchester this afternoon. Tell him to leave the van at the station.'

'Are you certain?'

He tucked the watch back into his waistcoat pocket. 'Certain as I can be. I'm not sending anyone back to get shot at.'

My mouth was dry, and I went into the kitchen for a glass of water. Grace was standing by the stove. 'I heard it all,' she said.

'Then you'd best get his case packed.'

'I'm going with him,' she said.

The water was so cold it made my throat ache. Water from the moors is usually too soft for pleasant drinking, but ours came from the new reservoir and it danced on the tongue.

'Where will you go?' I asked.

'Anywhere he says. He wants to marry me. Not that he has to. I don't care about that.' She chafed her hands as if they were chilled. 'I don't feel at odds with him like I do with other folk. I don't feel stupid.'

'Will you tell Father?'

'No. And don't you, either. I'll write to him.'

'He'll be upset.'

'No, he won't,' said Grace. 'If you think that, you don't know him at all.'

She packed a case for Harry and herself, and when she came downstairs my father gave her an envelope. 'There's fifty quid there,' he said. 'Tell him not to spend it all at once.'

'I'll tell him,' said Grace. She paused at the door, then turned and kissed each of us on the cheek.

'Fancy that,' said my father.

We watched her follow the line of the wall along the top meadow, then cross our neighbour's field to the road which led to the station. We heard the van splutter up the hill from the village and grind to a halt. When it started up again the hooter sounded twice, and I fancied I saw a hand wave from the window. We went back to sorting bricks for the path, but after a while we sat with our backs to the wall and watched the clouds sail across the valley trailing their shadows over empty fields. A train crossed the viaduct and pulled into the station. Passengers got in and out. Doors slammed, and finally it drew away to the south. My father glanced at his watch. 'Bang on time.'

'Grace has gone with him.'

'I thought she might have.'

'Don't you mind?'

'It's her life,' said my father. 'Harry's a good lad. You can't blame him for not wanting to get himself killed. Not in that bloody shambles.'

'She'll be missed, though. We'll need someone else to keep house.'

'Think on it, then,' said my father. 'It's about time you were wed.'

He stood up, his knee-joints cracking, and I followed him into the house. It was quite still, and from the living-room I heard the soft hammering of wings against the bars of the cage. The visiting finch flew into the garden, and I saw his rosy breast and black cap bobbing like a shuttle through the raspberry-canes.

My father unfastened the door of the cage, and the little hen hopped on to his finger. He lifted her out and held her like an offering to the sky. 'Go on, then,' he said. 'Go and find him.'

She crouched against his hand for an instant and then launched herself into the maze of green leaves. She was joined by the cock and, beating his wings to keep his balance, he mounted her. It was as quick as striking a match. He stepped off on to an adjacent branch, preened himself, then mounted her again.

Minutes later we heard the police car draw up outside the house, the thud of the door as it slammed shut and the crunch of George Marsden's feet up the path. The finches darted away, and we watched them until they were out of sight.

My father heaved a sigh which seemed to begin half-way between relief and regret.

'Right you are, then,' he said. 'Let's go and talk to George.'

Things

V. S. Pritchett

I WAS out early practising my putting on the lawn which I have brought pretty well to perfection. This was the first time I had had a chance to get out my clubs after a week of gales. They strike this tip of south-west England first, tear through the leaning trees and send the fields and hedges streaming and the steep hills bowling across the map into the Channel and take your mind and the tears in your eyes away with them. But now, as if the whole rumpus had not occurred, the sky was cloudless and as still as glass, and the only sounds were the tap of my club on the balls and the cries of the gulls ripping through the air. The young gulls must have hatched, and the parents were driving off the crows. Probably next day there would be sea fog. We don't live on land here, as my wife says, we live in weather. One lives from one hour to the next, as they turn into days and the weeks and the piled-up years we spent in Africa, Canada, Egypt and Hong Kong. On this quiet day last April Rhoda rang up. I remember it was the first time that we had been able to have breakfast outside.

As I say, I was out on the lawn and I heard the telephone ring. I am supposed to be retired, but the week rarely passes before I've had two or three calls from the London office, the dockyard or some Ministry about an oil-rig or a dry dock or asking me to go and serve on some commission of enquiry. I am a consultant now, called in when something goes wrong – stress mostly. I crossed the lawn. My wife was standing by an open window answering the call. Not in her usual calm practical way, but in a high, thrilled, rushing voice.

'Darling, how extraordinary! How marvellous! Where are you? What are you doing? Why didn't you write? We've been so worried about you. What are you doing . . .?' And so on, as she used to do when we first met and she was in love. She looked younger and warmer with every word. Then she saw me and waved me impatiently away.

'Not for you,' she said. 'Rhoda.'

Rhoda is her sister who lives in Italy. Miranda was, I supposed, shouting to be heard in the Mediterranean. She always shouts on an international call. But she was really proclaiming, in her emotional way, across time, and that is why she was looking so young. We haven't seen Rhoda since we went to Hong Kong and that must have been ten years ago and, frankly, it has been a relief. She has never been one to write – a Christmas card every year, of course, but nothing more.

When the long call came to an end Miranda stood staring over the fields into the sky and to the sea. Then she came back out of time when she saw me again.

I said: 'Has anything happened? Something wrong? It must have cost her a penny or two ringing from Italy.'

We often laughed at Rhoda's comic miserliness over small sums of money.

'She's not in Italy,' said Miranda, accusing Rhoda, me and the view, with one of her dramatic stares. 'She's on her way down from London. She's in Exeter. I've asked her to stay the night. She's sad the children are not here; she was longing to see them.'

There was a pause as her excitement died.

'She is incredible,' Miranda said. 'She said she didn't know they were both married. Yet I wrote to her. You saw the letter. She even sent them wedding presents.'

'Typical Rhoda; she lives in the future,' I said.

Miranda frowned at me.

'Be nice,' she pleaded.

I was thinking: I hope she's not bringing that awful man Sammy she's living with, that awful man with the wide trousers. But I checked myself. I retreated into a joke that goes back to the time when I first met Miranda and when Rhoda was no more than a child.

'I wonder', I said, 'what she *wants*,' pronouncing that word in Rhoda's baby-talk way when she was very determined, dwelling on it – "wawnt".

That call had opened up the past for Miranda and me.

'I bet she'll "wawnt" our house,' I added.

And Miranda said firmly: 'Well, she can't have that.'

We are very proud of our house. We are in our sixties, though Miranda does not look it – her hair is brown and has scarcely any grey – but the house has rejuvenated us. After working for so long abroad, living as we had to do in hotels, company bungalows and other people's furnished flats and villas, and with nothing of our own there, this is about the first time we have had a place that is really ours and with our own things. New sofas, beds, chairs, we are still as excited as if we were newly married. We came to live here because Miranda was born and brought up in this part of the country in a house called Lodge seventeen miles away, a place which had been in her family for something like a hundred years – more than that, I suppose. We have the portrait of her great-great-grandfather, 'the Trafalgar Captain', who retired from the Navy and bought the place after *that* war. The picture hangs in our drawing-room now. Lodge is where I first met the family during *our* war. In the invasion scare I was billeted in the stables: we were wiring the beaches and building those concrete strongpoints and pill-boxes on the coast. Miranda and I sometimes pass Lodge on our way to London. You can't see it from the road now because the trees and shrubberies are overgrown. You cannot even see the ludicrous stump of brick tower that her grandfather built at one end of the place, in a fit of pretension, for the house is no more than a plain square farmhouse of narrow slabs of brown and black stone. The trees darkened the large rooms even in Miranda's time, and the troops used to get scared of the squeaks of the branches scraping the slates at night. Miranda loved Lodge and was sad that the place, so settled and with windows that still for her seemed to hold the faces that had looked through them, was sold when her mother died. Rhoda detested it – or said she did.

Our own house is, I am glad to say, modern and pretty with its pink walls, and I have improved it. I am efficient in this kind of thing, and Miranda has furnished it with taste. Living here, we often say, is like having a second honeymoon. We live to ourselves and know hardly any of the summer people who come down, though I meet one or two on the golf course. Our children and grandchildren come in the summer. Thick walls of flowering shrubs ten feet high – which I keep well clipped – protect Miranda's garden where she is always working when she is not painting a little. Painting got her through the loneliness of being abroad. Here, since this is her own country, she isn't lonely and paints less. She says the light changes too fast for her now.

So Rhoda came to stay.

We both say still that we did not recognise Rhoda first of all except for her walk on the gravel drive. She trotted. She trotted like a busy little girl as she got out of the car and first went sniffing round it, peering in and seeing the doors were locked. She used to keep everything locked when she was a child. Then she stepped on to the lawn in the high-heeled shoes she always wore to give her height and stood back like an impertinent urchin staring at the house, counting the windows; she had always been a counting girl. Then, chin still lifted, her nose wriggled and she sniffed – a good sign with her: she admired the place! I was right: she was the historic Rhoda still 'wawnting', until plaintiveness quickly followed.

But she was not any of the series of Rhodas we had in memory of her, certainly not the Rhoda I had last seen about to leave my bank in London, ten years before when she was off to Italy. Like Miranda's, her hair was brown when she was a girl, but that day in the bank it was yellow and on it she was wearing a small black flower-pot hat. She had always been one for a fashion that had gone out, and with her smudged lipstick, her hit-or-miss eye-shadow she looked at that time like a widow who had not yet mastered the part. Naturally: she was unmarried. There was a man looking red-faced and hot from a funeral with her – the man with the trousers. (I will come back to Sammy later on.) But this was not the Rhoda we now saw on our lawn. We had expected sunburn, an Italian look. But instead her little face was scalded; she wore no make-up. The flower-pot hat had been replaced by a man's shabby brown beret tipped forward on her head, and from under it poured a long stream of hair, grey as fog, over her shoulders and down her back. She was wearing something like a striped football jersey and bright emerald pants, and she had a small belly full of impudence and authority. She looked like a witch out of a child's book. I did not say this to Miranda as we walked towards her, but I did say: 'Rhoda still wants justice.' (She was always saying in her quarrels with Miranda: 'It isn't fair. I want justice, Miranda.')

Rhoda trotted to us, the kissing began, and then abruptly she stepped back and considered us.

'You've grown a beard,' she mocked. I have a pointed white beard. 'You look pink and respectable.'

'Oh,' laughed Miranda. 'Not as respectable as he looks.'

'You see! ' cried Rhoda with glee and turning to me. 'She got her dig in.'

Rhoda has always lived by a few key words. After 'want' came 'digs'; she loved to see people getting 'digs' in at each other. The next word came out when I said 'Where's your suitcase?' and looked into the back of her car. A pile of old cardboard boxes and tied-up packages had been tumbled in. On top of them was a teapot, a radio, two umbrellas, a couple of pairs of slacks, an anorak, two tins of biscuits, Wellington boots and a stack of steel rods wrapped in canvas which looked like golf clubs. And a rolled sleeping-bag.

'I didn't know you played golf,' I said.

'No, that's my bed. I can't sleep in hotel beds. I always put it up on the floor. I stopped in Exeter on the way down.'

'Been making tea?' I said. There was a teapot on the floor.

'I picked it up in Taunton market,' she said. She had a plastic bag in her hand.

'Nothing in the car?' I said.

'No, those are my things,' she said, holding the bag tightly.

'Things' was another word that went back to her childhood. I remember the chest of drawers in her room at Lodge and – more important – one or two boxes, containing all her broken watches and dolls, strips of velvet or silk, patterns, knitting, sewing, badges, clips, combs, childish jewellery, letters, programmes, the crown of a hat she had once had, a mug, unused diaries and cracked snapshots, dozens of cotton-reels. No one in the family – certainly not Miranda or a maid – there were maids when she was a child – was allowed near the hoard. Once I remembered her mother saying: 'You must clear this mess up. What is the good of *one* stocking?' She held up the thing, and Rhoda snatched it from her, putting it into a cardboard box and sitting on it. 'It's mine.'

We were about to move into the house when she stopped and pointed to the white gate.

'Philip,' she said. 'I say! "Pebbles"! was that your idea?'

'It's the name of the house. What about it? Down this road there's "Breakers", "White Sands", "Sea Spray", "The Dunes".'

'Weird,' Rhoda mocked.

'I don't see anything weird in it,' I said. 'You have "Bella Vista" all over Italy.'

'Sammy and I live in a flat,' she said and then turned to Miranda and said: 'Sammy is my lover.'

'Yes,' said Miranda. 'Philip told me.'

'Lover' is not the last but it is the most important of Rhoda's key words. She did not live in time, as we did: the coming and going of lovers marked the calendar for her. We did not know many of Rhoda's friends but I cannot think of any man of whom she did not casually make this claim or, at any rate, did not pause to consider whether she might wish to make it at some time or other. Sammy seemed to have lasted longer than most.

'I wish you'd brought Sammy,' said Miranda. 'I've never met him, you know. You didn't leave him in Exeter, did you?'

'No, he's gone to Rome. I expect he's still in bed. He was fast asleep when I left.'

'I will get some tea,' I said.

'No. I want to see the house first. Everything,' said Rhoda, and she put on her glasses for the inspection.

I let Miranda take her. For an hour I could hear them going from room to room upstairs, talking and laughing. I went up at last to see how they were getting on. They came out of a bedroom and I pointed to the radiators and said: 'Have you shown Rhoda the bathrooms?' They ignored me. I went along to the first bathroom and, since they didn't follow, I flushed the lavatory.

Rhoda said: 'Why did you do that?'

'He loves doing it,' said Miranda. 'He'll never stop being an engineer.'

'Not like those lavatories at Lodge,' I called, 'where the pipes clanked all over the house and you thought it was coming down, or like that one in Cairo – that was the worst.'

'It's like a second honeymoon being here,' said Miranda – our phrase.

'I never had one. Everything else, but not that. I mean, you can't count Jeremy,' said Rhoda, walking slowly along the landing and peering at each print on the wall.

' "Poachers Netting Partridges at Night",' she read aloud. 'That was at Lodge. In the hall.'

We got down to the sitting-room; it was once two rooms and is now large, and from the two west windows there is a clear sight of the sea and the Pig Rock lying two miles out with its moustache of surf. Some days, when bad weather is coming, this rock seems to move in dark and near; on this afternoon it glittered and seemed farther away. It's the first thing I look at when I get up in the morning, better than a barometer. I mentioned this, but Rhoda, who had not taken

all her early lovers, 'He was impotent', to see how the Bulwers took that.

We shall have to stop that! I thought. Very embarrassing on a golf course; as bad as the time I was persuaded to take Rhoda on in our London office and she fell for Doggett on the Board and his wife asked Miranda to stop it. If she has come back to start those old larks, I thought, I'll have something to say and she won't like it.

But Rhoda was chattering on.

'Peter Ogbourne says prices have gone sky high since we sold Lodge.' And looking at a china cabinet in the room she said: 'You'd get five or six hundred for a piece like that. I gave Peter a lift to Plymouth. His car had broken down. He was going to a sale.'

'I don't think we are selling anything, are we, Miranda?' I said coldly.

Miranda said: 'Why don't we sit down?'

Rhoda studied the positions of the sofas and armchairs and then she looked closely at one of the chairs, which had a footstool half-concealed under it.

'My darling little stool,' she cried. She darted at it, kneeled down and pulled it out and sat on it victoriously. I have never seen an object 'bagged' so quickly in my life.

'Yes,' said Miranda, 'Granny's little stool.' And to me: 'Rhoda and I used to fight for it. Granny made us take turns.'

'Granny always cheated,' said Rhoda, dropping her mouth open and looking from one to the other of us to see if the 'dig' had got home.

What I remembered as I went out to get the tea-tray was Rhoda at the age of fifteen in school uniform sitting on the stool at Lodge before Miranda and I were married, staring at love, as we sat on a terrible prickly horse-hair sofa. And Rhoda saying 'Why don't you hold hands?' At fifteen she was a pest who followed us everywhere. She had just become very religious: one of the maids had converted her to the Plymouth Brethren. 'But, darling,' her mother said, 'they're not quite our class.' Her religious phase lasted until the second year of the war when the invasion scare came and soldiers were billeted in the stables. One of them, a Captain Blake, called her 'the pocket Cleopatra'. It was in her Plymouth Brethren phase that she once left the room, saying 'Sexual Intercourse is Damnation.' She loved the phrase because it shocked her mother.

I put the tray down. Rhoda gazed at the silver teapot and then shook a passing fancy out of her head.

'If I had married Jeremy Bulwer, I'd have had Lodge,' she said. And, picking up a scone, waved that at the room and said: 'Did you take all this to Africa?'

'No. Of course not. Most of it's new. We left one or two Lodge things with Philip's mother,' said Miranda. 'There wasn't much: the cabinet, the Trafalgar Captain, the secretaire. . . .'

'I suppose you took everything to Italy?' Miranda said. 'It would be easier.'

'Oh, no,' said Rhoda, biting her scone. 'We sold it all.'

'Everything when you went to live in the Square. . .,' Miranda began nervously.

'Yes, Sammy and I sold everything when we bought the hotel.'

'All of it? Oh, Rhoda!'

'We ought to have kept the silver,' Rhoda said. 'We'd have got ten times the price now. Money is money, isn't it? As Sammy says, no good hoarding. Things need a change. It cheers them up, he says.'

'It's cheered up the Captain coming here, I must say,' I said, pointing to the portrait. 'You couldn't see him at Lodge. We had him cleaned.'

Rhoda sniffed at the Captain. 'Imagine the life of his wife, polishing all that stuff, chained to it, while he was at sea,' Rhoda said.

'But you used to love *things* Rhoda,' said Miranda. 'It seems so sad, but I suppose it was sensible. There wouldn't have been room in your hotel.'

'We've sold the hotel,' said Rhoda. 'All those bloody tourists, taking photographs and talking about "art". It was too much for Sammy's nerves – I mean, the old people you get, always complaining about their washbasins and quarrelling with one another: some are quite mad. And the bells going all day.'

Miranda said in her discreet orderly way: 'We've never been quite sure what Sammy *does*. I do wish you'd brought him with you. What does he *do* now?'

Miranda had never quite believed my account of Sammy when I came back from our accidental meeting so long ago at the bank. What had struck me particularly in the young man was his trousers: his jacket was open and the trousers were braced high over his wide waist, almost to his ribs. He had black hair with a curl over his forehead and a lumpy, glistering, crimson face, and his fists, his nose, his lips were heavy: his body looked too full of blood, like a boxer's, a publican's or one of the security guards' at the bank. Rhoda said: 'I want you to meet Sammy. He's my lover.' They looked as though they had hired each other, and he came forward and said 'Pleased to meet you' in a confidential way that suggested 'This bird and I have just done a deal.' And he looked back shrewdly at the bank clerks at the main desk, as he might have glanced back at a bar when he was going to offer a new pal a drink.

'We are in a rush,' Rhoda said. 'We've only got half an hour to get to the airport. We're going to Italy.'

'S'right,' Sammy said.

Rhoda looked proudly amused by the disparity of their accents – a 'dig' at me, of course.

'Come on,' she said to Sammy, and he lazily followed her sharp steps out of the bank and called back: 'Be seeing you.'

One thing I was certain of: he was afraid of Rhoda.

Now, as Rhoda was passing her cup to Miranda, she said: 'He's got a nightclub now. It's much better for him. Poor Sammy, he's allergic to the sun in Italy. It upsets his eyes. He's short-sighted. He likes nightwork; he sleeps all day.'

I remembered how the hulking fellow blinked when he was introduced to me. I said to Miranda when I got home:

'Rhoda's short-sighted, too. They probably don't see each other.'

'We get a crowd,' Rhoda was saying now. 'Especially at the weekends.'

Her business – like words – brought to Rhoda's little eyes that miserly gleam the family used to tease her about at Lodge, which had evidently lasted: the clothes she was wearing looked cheap. But the plaintive drooping mouth of her 'wawnting' was not there. Her lips curled up happily when she talked of Sammy.

'Money is very necessary to Sammy, you know,' she said to me.

'We all need money nowadays,' I said.

'You don't understand, Philip,' she said. 'He needs it for his gambling.'

'Oh, Rhoda, you don't mean you've got a gambling club?' cried Miranda.

'He doesn't drink. He doesn't even drink wine in Italy. He doesn't mind if I do. He *needs* to gamble.' Rhoda added: 'Psychologically.'

'Oh, Rhoda! I don't know. Isn't that awful for you? I know they make money sometimes, but they lose it! It's lucky you haven't a family.'

'But I have!' Rhoda said. 'There's Sammy's little boy. He's sweet. He calls me "Mamita".'

'We didn't know Sammy was married before,' we said together.

'He wasn't. He had an Italian woman,' said Rhoda triumphantly.

And she sat back, looking from one to other of us with storyteller's glee. She sighed.

'How nice it is here. D'you remember how we used to go up the cliff to watch the baby seagulls? Will you take me, Philip, while I'm here?'

'I am sure Philip will take you,' said Miranda, 'when he's done his letters.'

I took the hint and went to my study. There is a photograph of an oil-rig being towed out to sea on one wall and a watercolour of boats in Hong Kong harbour – one of Miranda's – but all I could think of was Rhoda's long grey hair down her shoulders. 'She's mad. She's mad.' It was the usual tale of an old woman trying to look young, being bled for her money by a layabout. The scene in my bank kept racing across the page as I started to write a letter and had to give up. Perhaps Sammy had sent her over here to get money out of Miranda?

An hour went by and then Miranda opened my door and, looking back cautiously, said loudly: 'Are you ready to take Rhoda to see the baby seagulls while I start cooking?'

Miranda looked behind her and listened and then whispered: 'I think she's looking for a house.'

'Here? Oh, God! Not here?'

'She's on about starting an antique-shop. I believe she and Sammy are breaking up.' But she stopped, for we heard Rhoda's heels in the hall.

'He'd love to, Rhoda,' Miranda called.

Rhoda and I got into the car. When the sun goes down into the sea here it often sets off a firework display, sending out pink rockets all over the sky, but this evening there was no more than a slow, dull, yellowing light above a bank of low cloud that was coming in. The day was going and the sea was as flat as slate.

'It's going to be too late to see the baby seagulls,' I said as we slowed down at the turning to the cliff.

'I don't care whether I see them or not,' Rhoda said. 'Peter and I will see them tomorrow – Peter Ogbourne. I've got to get off early. I'm picking up Peter and we're driving to Falmouth. He's got another sale there. Let's go to Lodge.'

So all this talk of seagulls was a trick to get me to 'drop in' on the Bulwers. I was not going to have that.

'I was wrong just to pass it,' she said wistfully.

So the drive was to be a sentimental trip on a cloudy evening. There is something bemusing about the narrow roads in this part of the country. A stranger can easily get lost in them; they wind between banks of stone slabs and with high hedges on top of them so that you are tunnelling and see nothing of the country but, simply, sky. North, south, east and west vanish. At the sharp corners there are often signposts pointing to four ways with different distances for getting to the same village. Tourists laugh at them, forgetting these roads were built not from place to place, but from farm to farm. The only dramatic sight is the number of dead trees one passes, tall silver skeletons with their branching arms stuck up, like a preacher's.

Rhoda was counting the skeleton trees with excitement. She said: 'There is one at Lodge.'

'I'll slow down. I can't stop; it's a nasty corner,' I said, for I was still suspicious. 'You won't be able to see anything.'

'That's all right,' she said again. 'There's the dead tree. Just to feel myself passing it.' The sight contented her. And so very slowly we passed the gate of the overgrown drive.

The old concrete pill-box we built just inside the drive during the war was still there, but with nettles growing out of it now. The sight of that pleased Rhoda, too. She used to stand there watching us build it.

'I liked the war,' she said. 'It was fun. Very good for women.'

'Not for your mother or anyone with children,' I said. 'No more servants. They went into the factories.'

'That's what I mean,' she said. 'They got decent wages for once. Mother was hell to the village girls we had.'

'Women have a worse time now,' I said.

We got into the usual argument, but she rattled on until she suddenly stopped and said: 'D'you remember Captain Blake? He turned me out of the Tower. I was furious with him. . . . Putting a machine-gun post up in the Tower. Stupid idea. It was *my* room. I had all my things there. I think that's where I lost my Coronation mug.'

Her indignation died.

'Poor Captain Blake. Why did they *arrest* him?'

I could have said, 'You know why, Rhoda. Don't look so innocent,' but she carried on.

'I know he was rather – you know – but he really did *like*

little girls. He was only cuddly. He called me "the pocket Venus".'

I said I thought it was 'the pocket Cleopatra'.

'No,' said Rhoda fiercely. 'It was Venus.'

We had now passed the gate, thank God, and had gone beyond the wood at the end of what used to be the garden. She closed the window of the car and tidied her hair, spreading it carefully over her shoulders, looking like a witch again, and said: 'By the way, Peter is not my lover, you know. Actually I am not interested in sex anymore.'

This was the most startling remark I had ever heard Rhoda make.

'I didn't think he was,' I laughed. 'You've only known him a day.'

'Two days,' she said.

We were back in the maze of high-banked lanes and I put the headlights on.

'I showed the children to Peter,' she suddenly said. 'I've got them in the car.'

A home-going tractor, with no lights, came suddenly out of a blind side-turning when she said this and I had to brake suddenly.

'Bloody fool,' I called out. 'What do you mean – children?'

'The Captain's children – the picture with his wife. They're in the back of the car. I brought them with me. Peter says I ought to take them to Sothebys and get them valued; they'd fetch a good price. Did Miranda tell you, Sammy and I are going in for antiques? Not in Italy; Italy's finished.'

And then she said: 'I *saw* that in Exeter.'

She was talking to herself.

'Saw' was a word I had forgotten. It is really the most important. When Rhoda 'sees', she is having a sudden vision or revelation which comes into her mind out of the blue, driving out all calculation for the moment. I think it must have started in her religious phase and was something she got from the Brethren, something like 'a call'; but you hear a 'call'; you 'see' a vision. Miranda and I used to be distressed or angry about the mess she seemed to make of her life – those 'lovers' always left her, she did not leave them, and then her money obviously being thrown away on Sammy – it seemed to us – a bad end to it. What kept her going were these sudden 'seeings'.

'I don't know anything about shops. I'm an engineer. Don't shops require capital? I don't know anything about antiques.'

'But Peter does,' she said.

I knew what was going to happen as my headlights lit up our pink house. Rhoda would rush in to Miranda, alight with vision, and say that I said the idea was splendid.

That is almost what happened when I was getting the drinks and Miranda came in from the kitchen. Miranda and I exchanged helpless glances – 'What has she told you? What do you know?' What did Miranda mean when she had whispered that she thought Rhoda and Sammy were breaking up? Was anything really said? 'And what about this man Peter? What is going on?' Miranda was signalling. 'I don't know. Do you?' We were like actors sketching our way through lines to a plot which only Rhoda knew. I said, to forestall Rhoda: 'No baby seagulls.'

'We went to Lodge,' said Rhoda.

'Just passed it,' I said, to calm Miranda.

Rhoda paid no attention to us.

'I'll get the children,' she said and, carrying her drink with her, she went out to the car.

I said to Miranda quickly: 'The Captain's children. She's going to sell the picture.'

Rhoda returned, holding her glass high in one hand and carrying the picture which was nearly as tall as herself. It was wrapped in old sacking and roughly tied. She put it against a chair and swallowed her drink. Then she knelt down and started picking at the string. Bits of the dirty sacking made a mess on the carpet. I tried to pick it up. I hate a mess in a room. We saw the picture at last.

Unlike our portrait of the Trafalgar Captain, this picture was much larger – we always said that was why Rhoda had chosen it. It was exactly as it had been at Lodge – blackened by age, which made the faces small and yellow. The Captain's wife was sitting on a stone bench, under a tree, and with her were three little girls in once white dresses with blue ribbons, one child looking down at a dog. A country scene but, rather absurdly, the painter had put the mast of a ship in the background. Our Captain at any rate looked rosy and alive; his wife and family were peaky and stiff like dolls. Rhoda came to business at once. Peter had seen it and said: 'It's a Primitive. Primitives fetch a price.' What was certain, he said, was that it would fetch three times as much if the Captain were sold with it.

'Rhoda! What a sad thing to do with a family thing. Sell the children! You don't mean it,' Miranda said.

Rhoda watched our faces.

'Well, I can tell you this: we're not selling the Captain, are we, Miranda?' I said. Let Rhoda sell what she liked. My temper was rising at the sight of Rhoda proposing to sell our things under our noses and turning our house into a sale-room. Rhoda went one better.

'I'll sell them to you, if you like,' Rhoda said, dropping her mouth open like a haggler.

'We don't want them,' I said. 'Do we, Miranda?'

'But, Rhoda, the two pictures are not by the same painter,' Miranda said. 'You can see that by the signatures. The children were done by some local man – Barnes or something. Ours is a Drummond.'

I admired Miranda's quickness. Rhoda was startled, but shook the idea out of her head.

'Peter says it's a Drummond,' she argued.

'Soon settle that. Look at the signature.'

It was illegible, but on the back was a label saying: *Flora Barnes, Falmouth*.

Miranda said shrewdly: 'Does Sammy want you to sell it?'

Rhoda put on an airy manner and gave one of her dry cackles.

'Sammy doesn't know I've got it here,' she said. 'He'd go

off her beret, did not reply. She was standing still in the
room which I consider Miranda's masterpiece: she ought to
have been a decorator, she has such a gift for colour. This
room had cost us quite a lot of money. Rhoda was counting
again. In that jersey and those terrible emerald trousers, she
stood out like a gypsy. Quick as a bird, she picked out the
one or two family things that had come to us from Lodge.
She stared at the portrait of 'the Trafalgar Captain' over the
fireplace and said suddenly: 'I looked in on old George
Ogbourne in Exeter.'

'We wondered why you stopped in Exeter,' Miranda
said.

'You should have come straight through. Who is George
Ogbourne?'

'Oh, you know him,' said Rhoda. 'He used to be at
Raddles, the auctioneers who sold Lodge when the Bulwers
bought it. Those auction people make the money! He went
in for antiques. He remembers *you*, Miranda. And he remembered me. "Let me see, you must be Rhoda," he said. He's
getting on. His son Peter runs the business now. He knows
the Bulwers. You didn't tell me that Jeremy Bulwer had
married again when his wife died, that fluffy little thing.
What is the new one like?'

'We don't know the Bulwers,' I said. 'I just see him at the
golf course sometimes. Very bald.'

'But Jeremy was my first lover!' she said, forgetting us
and the room for a moment, and she took a step or two,
looking at her feet as if talking to one foot and then the
other, plotting. And then said sentimentally: 'I think I'll
drop in at Lodge while I'm here. For old times' sake.'

This silenced us. I know that thirty years have passed and
that, thank God, Rhoda's love-affairs are no business of
ours. But this was too near home. I could just imagine
Rhoda 'dropping in' at Lodge and getting in a sizeable 'dig',
saying what a funny thing it was, Jeremy had been mad
about her and they'd run off to London when he was
engaged to his first wife. In the end the silly girl had taken
him back. And then adding loudly, what she used to say of

out of his mind. I packed it up when he was out at the club with some woman of his.'

Her eyes went into slits of pleasure at the memory of her trick.

Miranda said: 'Have you left Sammy?'

'I'll never leave Sammy,' Rhoda said. 'And Sammy won't leave me. When he finds out I've got the picture and gets my letter about Peter and the prices things fetch, he'll be over on the next plane. Sammy will do anything for money. He'll bring the little boy.'

She went into a brisk dream.

'Gamblers love children, and that woman hates them.'

'You mean and bring the – er – lady?'

Rhoda, Sammy and his mistress – on our doorstep!

'No,' said Rhoda. 'I don't mind what women he has, but he's had this one long enough. I know how to manage Sammy.'

Neither Miranda nor I could think of anything to say. Rhoda held out her glass, and I gave her another drink. Rhoda saw that her proposal had failed, and when her 'visions' fail she always throws them away. She looked down at her shoes thoughtfully and said in her sly and deedy voice, very slowly sketching her way into a new idea: 'I actually don't think I will sell the picture when Sammy gets here,' she said. 'I haven't any children of my own. The boy is rather sweet. He likes the picture; he thinks they're mine.'

And then she said shrewdly: 'And Peter says when you go in for antiques it's always a good thing to have something you won't sell in a shop.'

And Rhoda knelt on the floor and began to put the picture back into its sacking. I helped her.

I said: 'I can't see Sammy in an antique-shop. You can't sleep all day in a shop.'

'I'll run the shop,' she said. 'I'm going to talk to Peter tomorrow. He might come in with us. They'll get on; they're both keen on money, and he's younger than Sammy. That'll keep Sammy awake.'

We both shouted with laughter, and Rhoda was surprised for a moment and then looked very clever. She went to sit on the stool.

Miranda said that dinner was ready, and as she went into the kitchen called back: 'Is Peter married, Rhoda?'

'God, no,' Rhoda called back and looked at me, suggesting that there was something stupid in our condition.

We went to eat in the alcove at the end of the room. When we were served Rhoda put her head down close to her plate and looked up to see what our forks were putting into our mouths.

There was no more talk about pictures or Sammy or Peter, but we laughed about old times at Lodge – the soldiers there, how kind Captain Blake was to her the night Plymouth was bombed and how Miranda had found her sitting on the Captain's knee in her nightgown and she had fallen asleep and had a terrible dream that she was struggling with Miranda in the sea.

Rhoda said: 'I thought you were drowned. I was trying to save you.'

Miranda said drily: 'And you brought me a cup of tea every morning for a week afterwards. I wondered why.'

'It was weird,' said Rhoda, ignoring this. 'Mother was so upset. I was only *talking* to poor Captain Blake. He wasn't my lover.'

'I should hope not, at that age,' said Miranda.

'He was after *you*,' said Rhoda, 'but you had Philip.'

'How ludicrous you are,' said Miranda.

'You see,' said Rhoda to me. 'She's guilty. I still can't see why they arrested him. Actually Blake was impotent,' Rhoda said with pride. 'He told me.'

'That's enough, Rhoda,' I said.

She looked mischievously at me, but obeyed.

There was no more fuss until bedtime came. She insisted on having her travelling bed put alongside the empty bed in the spare bedroom and when it was there she complained that it blocked the way to the window. She said that what she really wanted was to sleep in the drawing-room because she didn't want to disturb us. We protested, but she said she always got up at five and if she stayed with people she always left before they got up. She never ate breakfast. 'I've got my own teapot,' she said. She said she had a long drive before her, to pick up Peter. There was more trouble about the bed than about anything else in her visit. We gave in and brought the thing downstairs. There were trips back and forth to the car outside for her clock, her face things, her tissues, her toothbrush, her combs. Then she wanted a needle and cotton to mend the lining to her beret which, it turned out, was Sammy's.

So we left her on the sitting-room floor. In our room I said: 'Sammy must be a saint to live with a woman like that. What did she tell you?'

We talked and talked in low voices half the night. Sometimes we stopped to listen.

'She does worry me,' Miranda said. 'Did you think I was beastly to her when she was a child? She looks so awful.'

'I don't think so. Little things make her happy.'

'I do hope she's comfortable,' Miranda said.

Several times I got out of bed and looked out of the window: at three o'clock the light from the drawing-room was shooting out in squares and triangles on the lawn.

I woke early, leaving Miranda asleep, and when I got downstairs the drawing-room door was open. Rhoda had gone. I had woken early because the seagulls woke me up, and I had had an alarming thought about the Trafalgar Captain. I was relieved to see he was still hanging on the wall. I went to the front door. The car had gone but on the doorstep there was Granny's little stool, propped up against the foot scraper. Had she thought of taking it? Had she forgotten or changed her mind?

Rhoda's voice buzzed in our ears in the next few days. She did not telephone. She did not write. Months have gone by without news. I suppose we shall hear at Christmas. Miranda thinks Rhoda is very much like one or two of the old village people here who seem to be made of weather rather than of flesh and blood. They like living in their fancies and their 'seeings', trying out their lives in the air, trying their feelings on the market, shrewdly watching the bidders.

'She was trying out herself and her ideas on us,' Miranda said. 'Crystal-gazing like a gypsy. Making up her mind about Sammy.'

I don't know. Six months after she left, that Peter Ogbourne fellow came to the house, touting for antiques, and I sent him away with a flea in his ear, but we did ask him about Rhoda.

'Very kind old lady,' he said politely. 'She gave me a lift to Plymouth.'

'I thought she was giving you a lift to Falmouth,' I said.

'The funny thing is, I've never been to Falmouth in my life,' he said.

'She said something about showing you a picture of children – a Primitive.'

'Not me. It must have been the other dealer. Or my father,' he said. 'But she did give me your address.'

Old Tom

Celia Dale

THE trees stand close together at the top of a hill. The hill slopes down to crisscrossing tarmac paths, then down again and on to the limits of the common. The trees cluster, bare-trunked up from the bare earth – nothing will grow beneath them – branches, too, almost bare now, for it is the beginning of autumn.

The trees stand black in the darkness; there is no sound. Birds sleep, small creatures do not come here but live and forage in the gorse and scrub of more sheltered areas. Beneath and beyond the hill and the grass the pinkish glow of the city seems to draw all life from the empty slopes. There are only the trees, bare in the darkness, standing close to each other, rough-barked, old, weathered.

One of them is a man. He stands close among the closest trees, still as a tree, tall and straight as their trunks. He must stand so, shielded by them, or Dad will catch him. He wears an old army greatcoat, its buttons long gone, tied about the waist with string. The glow from down there is from the kitchen; he's safe behind the cupboard door if he don't move. Under the greatcoat is an old jacket, a ravelled pullover, a shirt grey once and now; under that, leather-brown skin, encrusted dirt that stirs in the creases. If he don't move, Dad'll think he's safe asleep. Over his shoulder hangs a battered airline bag, its zipper broken; PANAM, it says. At his feet lolls a supermarket's plastic bag; it is stuffed with newspapers, bits of food, old socks, his army paybook, a cutting showing King George VI taking the salute soon after VE-Day. Treasures. Dad mustn't find them.

There are no socks inside the stained plimsoles, but he

does not feel the earth's cold seeping through. He must not stir. Beneath a hat, wetted and battered out of shape, merged with the hair that straggles beneath it, Old Tom's gaunt face is alert. Dirt lies in its wrinkles and the stubble of his chin, but the bones are bold still. He has most of his teeth. His eyes, in their deep sockets, are sharp. When Dad slams the back door it will be safe to move. Not till.

In the morning the woman prunes ramblers. It is early yet, she knows, but they have got so overgrown now that her husband is no longer here to deal with them. He loved pruning roses. Nothing else, certainly not the lawn. That she could manage, but the roses. . . . Ruthless, she knows; cut right down and they will come again. But, knowing death now, she cannot bring herself to kill. Death's sting is here all right – in the worm, the slug, the aphid, the straggling sucker; the empty rooms. Room. Her room now.

Cut, snip, be ruthless. Life will come again in the roses. Not in the house.

There is a movement by the wall. She turns her head. An old black cat has jumped down on to the flower-bed and stands frozen at the sight of her. His fur is shabby, one ear is flat and ragged; his eyes in his wide black mask are lime-green and stark with shock.

They stare at one another. She should clap her hands at him, for cats dig holes in gardens. He stares, unblinking.

'Well, cat?' she says quietly.

Still staring, his shock abates. Tension, but not wariness, leaves his bony frame. Averting his green gaze, he begins to move, one paw at a time, away through the michaelmas daisies. His tail twitches – she can see now that its tip is not quite straight, broken at some time. Paw by slow paw he turns away, aware of every possibility of terror, rigid with dignity. He is lame in his hindleg but it moves easily, long forgotten. He reaches the fence and, suddenly swift, squeezes through out of sight.

The woman smiles. Sighs. Life. She abandons the roses and goes inside.

*

When the weather is fine Old Tom stays close to the common. He knows the dells and spinneys, the hollows under the viaduct by the pond, the wooden shelters by the sports ground, the many litter-bins in which a variety of food scraps can be found, old shoes sometimes, even torn clothing. With his two bundles beside him he sits for hours on a seat on the hillside below the night-time wood, above the spread city. No one disturbs him. People sit on another seat, for he looks forbidding and he smells. Sometimes a gang of boys will jeer at him. 'What's in the bag, Dad? Won the pools, Dad?' He looks at them with his innocent eyes. 'Where's your ma, Tom? Your ma's a whore, Tom. Your dad in the nick, Tom?' His eyes grow wild and he tries to rise, mumbling and waving his ragged arms. Afraid, the boys run off. 'Go piss yourself, Dad!' they shout over the grass. He shuffles his bags together, trembling, and moves away down the hill. He will be strapped for pissing himself; the orphanage master will take no excuses.

Down the hill, where the roads are, he makes for the bus terminus. There is a shelter there and the bus crews pay no attention to him if he sits there hour after hour. Sometimes he even stretches out on the bench, his bundles a pillow, and sleeps; but passengers object, expecially if it is raining. 'Come on, Dad, on your way.' Kindly or angrily, the inspectors know him. 'You can't doss here, Dad. Get off to the Haven.'

The Haven is down the street, a battered three-storey terrace house with bare floors and shabby scarred furniture. Young men and a few young women cook for and listen to the men and some women who drift in from the pavements. There is hot soup and pies; tea can be brewed in the scarred kitchen; wine and meths are surreptitiously slurped in the lavatories or the backyard or the dormitories after dark and instantly confiscated if discovered. No one is turned away; you can get a bed there for nothing.

Old Tom has tried it. It is not for him, even in the rain. They're all thieves there. Sleep with your treasures under your head, they're still thieves. Vera's ring, and her picture, where'd they go, eh? Never sold it, though it was nine-carat, hung on a string round his neck. Gone. Years ago when he first started wandering. Found his way about, roads, settlements, handouts. Soup-kitchens, coffee-stalls, wild men and women on bomb-sites, bonfires. Thieves. Where'd her picture go, then? In a little gold frame. Safe in his battle dress pocket all those years and then gone from his bags at one of them havens. She'd not like it. 'You're a softie, Tom. You need to look out for yourself. Stick up for yourself, Tom. I'll stand by you, Tom.' Where'd it gone, eh, and her ring? All thieves.

When the weather is fine he goes on past the bus terminus to the bulldozed site where the builders are coming. There are caves and crannies here, old foundations, cellars, passages. Weeds of great beauty have flourished here and make a cover better than houses. And there is food. People, old women mostly, bring and leave food there for the cats which have bred and gone wild here. They bring it in newspapers or cartons or on tin plates. Fresh food, fish all cooked or out of tins, bits of good meat.

Old Tom watches from a wrecked cellar door, merged in the willow-herb. The cats squat watchfully; they know it is time. Their tails twitch, their eyes do not blink. In a sly wave of fur they move out towards the women unloading their food, waiting till they are gone before streaking down to it. Rising and towering, Old Tom scatters all but the fiercest. The old tom holds his ground, hunched over the news-paper, eyes glaring, growling a spiralling yowl.

Old Tom respects him. Each eats.

Through the autumn the woman looks out of her windows and often sees the old cat limping across her grass. He goes unhurriedly, with an eye to the house but no fear. Sometimes he pauses, and through the glass they regard each other. She makes no movement, and after a moment he goes on, dot-and-carry, the fur over his thin ribs dull, his ear squashed, his tail bent at the tip.

It is a warm November; the french window is open. For

some days she has put a saucer of milk where it might catch his eye but she has not seen him. Now, sitting inside, trying to answer the letters that still come to her praising her husband, she sees the old cat crossing the grass.

She stills. He pauses. His eyes search, his blunt nose sniffs. Sniffs. It is near, luxury. Slowly, close to the ground, ears flat, he approaches. Sniffs. Looks about, green eyes hard. Hunches, begins to lap. Pink tongue in and out like the tick of a clock. Pause, take care, make sure. All well, hunch, lap. Lick the saucer clean. And again. Rise. Lick lips, twitch tail, give a last look up through the glass where the woman watches. Turn and limp leisurely away.

The woman smiles.

December is wet, January cold. The old women do not come so often to the building site, and the cats are less easy to disperse. People do not walk so often on the hills of the common, and the litter-bins contain little but paper and plastic. There is soup and a pie at the Haven, but more people, too. They crowd him. Get your fucking arse off me legs, Tom; we'll be ashore in a minute. Christ they've got our range. Hey, Corp, Corp, give us some room, for fuck's sake; your bleeding pack's in me face. I'll drown in the shallows; I'll sink in me fucking boots; I'll die in the sand, in the dunes, in the scrub. . . . Where's Vera's ring, eh? Where's her photo? Thieves, all thieves.

In the cold dusk he prowls. Silent in his dirty plimsoles, grey as the twilight, he explores dustbins and garbage-sacks. In the back entries to restaurants there are often treasures – half-eaten chicken-joints, hamburgers, bread, cold chips. An apple pie, mouldy; bruised fruit. In cans, dregs of strange fluids. Drinking-fountains are turned off now to save freezing, but there are ponds.

Silently, warily, Old Tom raises the dustbin lid. There are peelings and rinds, empty tins. From the side of the house a light shines out on to the path where he stands; he can see a half-loaf of bread, harmlessly moulded, and a mutton-bone still with meat on it. Eyes bright at the treasure, he bends his gaunt grey bundle of body towards it, delicately probing, decently, without greed.

A door opens and the woman steps out.

For an instant they stare at each other, frozen, she a looming shape dark against the bright interior, he a grey ghost, wild and predatory. She catches her breath; he gives a kind of mumbling shout, then turns and blunders away out into the street, dropping the dustbin lid as he goes. She stands, shaken for a moment, her heart thumping. Then steps down and replaces the lid on the dustbin; goes back into the house.

As the weather gets colder the cats on the building site decrease. The weak ones have died or been killed – there are rats, dogs and cars as well as stronger cats. Cold and damp undermine the remainder, and influenza creeps in. But the old tom survives. He is not so lean now, and his fur has a gloss on it. His tail is as bent, his limp as bad – worse, for the damp affects it; but each day, when the woman meets his green gaze through the french window, her heart swells. Slowly she opens the window wide enough for his entry. He steps back, his square black mask with its squashed ear studying her. Then, cautiously, he steps in. Just inside is a saucer of milk. Without looking about, he hunches and begins to lap. The woman goes quietly out of the room, and when she returns he is sitting, bent tail wrapped over his forefeet, waiting for what she has brought.

She places it before him. He hunches and eats, rapidly, noisily, flicking his head from side to side. Slowly she reaches out and slowly, slowly strokes her hand over his bony shoulders, his lean ribs, to his stern. He growls but does not cease from eating. At first, weeks ago, she dared not touch him. Even now she dare not touch his head. But this one slow caress she is now allowed while he chews and licks and swallows down, scours the plate, transfers to finish the milk, and at last, replete, sits up and, with precise ritual delicacy, begins to wash.

She watches him from her chair. Ears, mask, paws,

forelegs; back legs, claws deftly sieved, tight black balls and pink anus fanatically cleansed; face again, whiskers, ears. Lips licked, green gaze at last serenely meeting hers. A rise, a stretch front and back, a requesting glance. She rises and opens the french window. With a flick of his tail the old tom goes out into the darkness.

'Why not stay with us for a bit, Tom?' asks the young man in charge of the soup and the pies.

Tom just stares.

'It'd be best for your chest, you know, now the winter's come on. Just for the dinners and a bed?'

Tom doesn't answer.

'You could go where you liked in the day, you know that, Tom. You'd be your own master just as you like. Just look on us as your base, like?'

Base was where you were before and where you came back to after. Clanking, rough, sodden, harsh, crush, noise, boots, metal, noise, crush. Basement, with the house in powder and chunks on top of it, stairs still intact but all lies about being safe there. Nothing to see after, the rubble mostly all cleared, just the stairs still showing but empty, the feel of his boots and his pack and the cap on his head as he stood there. 'Sorry, lad. Got compassionate, have you? There's nothing more I can tell you. Tried the Town Hall? A nasty incident, this was. Still, he knows he's beat now and no mistake.'

Can't stay at the Haven, not under a roof. Only safe under sky. And all thieves. Where's Vera's photo, then? And her ring? Thieves.

There is little cover now on the common. The leaves have all fallen, the bushes are sparse. The shelter by the sports ground is locked up and the seat in the bus-terminus hut has been removed in order that no one shall sleep on it. The building site has been fenced off.

He sits on a bench by the lifts at the Underground station sometimes; the staff leave him alone, but the passengers look at him angrily and make him afraid. It is closed soon after midnight. Like a grey gaunt tree he makes his way silently back to the common, the brim of his rotting hat sagging over his stubbled face, his coat flapping below the waist-tied string, his bags of treasures bulging at his knees. Beneath the hat his eyes peer out, wild and blank and innocent. Behind the door Dad won't see him. He'll be strapped if he pisses the bed. Where's Vera's ring, eh? And her photo?

The old cat finishes. Sits up, washes his face and paws. She fears that his fur has lost some of its gloss, and he is wheezing a bit through his black nose. But he has drunk all his milk, eaten almost all his liver, and under her hand his spine rises slightly in acknowledgement of her caress.

Now, wheezing, he does not go through the whole ritual of the wash but sits for a moment, motionless. Then lifting his black mask to her, he gives her a long unblinking stare. His eyes are green as jade, and within them and their micraculous lenses she believes, with a surge of joy, that she sees love. They stare at each other, timelessly. Then he gets up, stretches, turns his head; she opens the door for him. He steps out, stiffly; and slowly, limpingly, moves off across the snow. His paws leave little holes.

She never sees him again.

VAGRANT FOUND DEAD

The body of Thomas Bradshaw, 76, was found on Northfield Common on Wednesday. Bradshaw, of no fixed address, was a familiar figure in the locality and was affectionately known as Old Tom by householders and social workers. An inquest returned a verdict of death from natural causes.

Flora's Lame Duck

Harold Acton

NOBODY knew where he had sprung from, and indeed there was something spectral about his limping after Flora in the backstreets of San Frediano, for he seldom appeared with her in the Via Tornabuoni where he would have been conspicuous. Alabaster-pale with piercing jet eyes and a mop of raven hair, he might have been Flora's son by a Latin lover.

It was rumoured that Flora had rescued him from a concentration-camp when she was working for the Red Cross at the end of the last world war, that he had been left an orphan stricken with polio, but he was too self-effacing to kindle much curiosity among Flora's frivolous acquaintances. At her cocktail parties he kept aloof from the crowd, impassive and immobile, if he happened to be in the room.

'Ugo is very shy,' she explained. 'Though not socially inclined, he needs to be near me.'

His mournful eyes followed Flora as she poured out drinks for her guests. Now and then he would limp towards her and whisper something in her ear. She smiled at him with gracious condescension. Flora had always been gregarious: at certain hours she liked to be surrounded by laughing chattering people. Which made it all the stranger that she should have taken so taciturn a protégé to live with her. One could hardly imagine that they had much in common. A maternal sympathy perhaps, for at nineteen Ugo still seemed adolescent.

'Like something the cat has brought in,' remarked her old crony Ronald Lipson with his usual malice. 'Makes me shudder. But one must put up with Flora's charities.'

Feeling sorry for that fish out of water, I joined him in his corner by the Japanese screen, but he was difficult to engage in conversation. When I introduced myself as a school-friend of Flora's all he could say in Italian was: 'Isn't she beautiful? The Lord has been merciful to me. She is my guardian angel.'

In her early forties Flora was still slender and girlish in her movements, simply yet stylishly clad without ornaments. Her carefully made-up face produced an impression of modern sophistication (Paris, London, New York) rather than of beauty. Having divorced a rich alcoholic husband, she took up various charitable works to assert her indi-viduality. It was assumed that Ugo belonged to that cat-egory. Flora's charities were personal yet selfless: she went out of her way to find congenial occupations for the dis-abled and underprivileged despite a distaste for physical contact with them. It was not easy to conceal her horror of the deformed. Elmer Stoddard, the one man she deeply loved, was married in New York, but his wife was suffering from an incurable disease and he had not the heart to abandon her. The specialists predicted that she could not last much longer. She was kept alive on sedatives.

Elmer implored Flora to be patient. 'We shall soon make up for lost time,' he assured her. All the time they were separated was lost for Flora; only her charities helped her to fill the great gap. It seemed cruel to hope for his wife to die, but in her predicament euthanasia would be a bless-ing.

Flora had been tempted to linger in New York for Elmer's sake until her frustration became intolerable. There was but little consolation in casual assignations, for Elmer, being full-blooded, attempted to make love to her whenever they met. The image of his bedridden wife hovered malignantly between them, and Flora suspected that she had the clair-voyance of the dying. A conventional believer in matri-mony, she would not yield to Elmer's entreaties for a premature consummation. So she reconciled herself to more anxious waiting. Meanwhile she decided to return to

Florence where she had struck roots with her former husband before the war.

Her Florentine friends clasped her to their bosoms, and those among them who had been ardent Fascists welcomed her, oblivious of bygone differences. The most ardent had been Anglo-American countesses who had deified the Duce as a symbol of heroic virility: some of them still cherished his photograph in secret. Several had been impoverished by the war, and these were the most eager to entertain her at their country estates which, after an esurient fortnight in England, seemed to be flowing with milk and honey.

Flora threw open her spacious apartment above the Arno to her polyglot coterie with the profuse hospitality of her pre-war period. None could forget those parties where so many marriages had been arranged, and again Flora revelled in the role of matchmaker. She had found husbands for spinsters and wives for bachelors – another reason for her warm reception by couples to whose infants she had been a fairy godmother. Seeing her again immaculate and unchanged, they hoped she would persevere on behalf of their offspring. The younger generation looked towards America as the goal of their ambitions. They had long been deprived of jazz, and the records Flora had brought from Manhattan excited their naïve enthusiasm. But the nostalgic tunes of the thirties were still the favourites with Flora's generation. Again, as before the war, an undulating group besieged the piano where Ronald Lipson regaled them with the lyrics of Cole Porter and Noël Coward. Ronnie knew most of them by heart and he sang them with the right intonations while others joined the chorus. Flora was reminded poignantly of Elmer when he crooned Gershwin's 'The Man I Love'.

It was the return of a Lady Bountiful who could solve everybody's problems except her own – her engagement to a man still tethered to a dying wife, and her subsequent responsibility for a limping waif.

Though he had been cured of polio, Ugo was morbidly conscious of his deformity. He feared that Flora was ashamed of being seen with him.

'I feel I'm a terrible encumbrance,' he told her.

'Nonsense, you should be thinking of a career. At your age there are so many to choose from. When you have chosen you may count on my assistance.'

In feeding and clothing him and sending him to study English at the British Institute she hoped he would discover a congenial profession. He had a talent for drawing which she encouraged by introducing him to a couple of artists who invited him to their studio and allowed him to draw from their models. Flora supplied him with abundant painting materials, delighted that he had found an innocuous hobby. Tactfully she respected his unwillingness to display his first efforts. 'You may show them to me when you feel you have something to be proud of,' she said.

'I should like to paint your portrait,' he replied, 'but I'm not good enough yet. I want to pour my love into the picture like the Mediterranean flowing into the Atlantic.'

Flora smiled as he prattled on with glittering eyes. He made sketches of her while she sat over her embroidery, and she would have been astonished at the result, for to her head and shoulders he added a naked figure with pear-shaped breasts and a forest of pubic hair interwined with tendrils of ivy and bulbous lilies.

Considering her affection for Florence, Flora was strangely indifferent to the visual arts, though she had a vague penchant for artists in general. Ugo hummed happily over his sketchbook. Ever and anon he moistened his large lips with a pointed tongue, and his black eyes scrutinised her so intensely that Flora was disconcerted. It had not crossed her mind that he might fall in love with her, but gradually she was forced to realise that this was happening. Never having experienced intimacy with a woman, he was peculiarly susceptible to Flora's attractions. 'You are so beautiful,' he sighed, 'it makes me despair. I feel like a worm beside you.'

'Don't be silly,' she replied. 'You're simply sweet but you are a baby compared to me. And I have no pretence to beauty.'

'You have been so kind to me, too kind. You have shown me a new world. How can I express my gratitude? Have you guessed how deeply I love you?'

'Be sensible, Ugo. Remember your age and mine, think of the difference.'

Ugo's eyes filled with tears. 'I cannot feel the difference, except that I'm a cripple.'

'You should regard your lameness as a distinction. Many famous people have been lame. Lord Byron for instance.'

As he had never heard of Byron, Flora gave Ugo a volume of his poems. No social introduction could have been as effective. He pored over the poems with rapture, and Byron became a cult. Now he wore an open shirt with his velveteen jacket and attempted to emulate his hero by learning to swim in the Arno. He developed his breast-stroke rapidly and while swimming forgot his deformity. Though his black eyebrows were gathered together above his nose, he fancied that his features resembled those of the poet.

Flora's friends noticed a marked improvement in Ugo's physique when she took him to Forte dei Marmi for the summer. She had rented a small villa with a garden near the sea where she could indulge in the same social round as in the city within easy reach of canasta-playing neighbours. Ugo clung to her in private but in public he remained equally remote with his Byronic pose of vague mystery and disdain. People might think what they pleased, but nothing Ugo said could compromise their relationship. He stood discreetly in the background, a *cavalier servente* at Flora's beck and call.

'After the hell she went through with her husband it's nice for Flora to have a young creature in attendance.'

'But what a creature! I wouldn't trust him round the corner. Half-boy, half-man, and not enough of either. He's getting a bit above himself. Flora gives him too much rope.'

His presence, even in the background, irritated the men who wanted to flirt with her. Which suited Flora, determined to be faithful to Elmer in thought, word and deed. Apart from assurances that he was alive and well, Elmer's letters brought little solace while his wife was kept barely alive by the miracles of modern medicine. In spite of her sociable routine at Forte, Flora found it increasingly difficult to be patient. Elmer embodied her ideal of a robust compatriot whose supreme sanity she could always bank on. His extreme wholesomeness was perhaps his principal charm: his very sweat was incense to her nostrils. In his last letter he had quoted Walt Whitman: 'I am to think of you when I sit at night alone, I am to wait, I do not doubt I am to meet you again, I am to see to it that I do not lose you.' Elmer's was the 'robust American love' celebrated by Whitman. Flora would fly back to New York as soon as he summoned her after the funeral. Both she and Elmer would be rejuvenated by a peripatetic honeymoon. Elmer had never been to Italy and Flora looked forward to acting as his guide and mentor.

Ugo was never mentioned in her letters, though he monopolised more of her attention than she cared to admit even to herself. During the summer at Forte they swam together all morning and lay on a strip of sand with towels and rugs, novels and magazines and a picnic-basket. Flora read in English to Ugo and he read in Italian to her, with playful interruptions and dissertations. In the afternoon Flora relaxed for a siesta under a mosquito-net in her cool shuttered bedroom while Ugo sat outside on the terrace under a canvas awning. Now and then he crept indoors to peep at her. He was restless, and the sight of her made him more so. As he was barefooted Flora could not hear him while he stood gazing at her with bated breath. Her eyes were blindfold while his gloated on the curves of her naked body. He longed to leap under the net and snuggle in beside her, but he crept stealthily out of the room with all his senses on fire. To melt into that sumptuous flesh had now become his obsession. He staggered back to the beach to cool himself in the sea, but the salt water failed to calm his raging fever. He resolved to keep away from Flora at siesta-time lest he could not resist the impulse to ravish her. It was difficult enough to control his emotion when she sat beside him.

'What's the matter, dear?' she asked with tender concern.

'I'm afraid you would not understand.'

'Aren't you happy here? Tell me what is upsetting you.'

'I'm only too happy to be with you, I can't express it. But I want more love than you could give a wretch like me. I'm afraid I'm repulsive to you.'

'You are mistaken, Ugo. Just look at yourself in the mirror.'

'I can only look at you, Madonna Flora. Every day you become more beautiful. And you are all I have in the world.'

'Nonsense, dear. At your age the world is your oyster.' She patted his cheek maternally.

He seized her hands and kissed them, and she could not help noticing the bulge below his belt. The sudden realisation that his senses were inflamed embarrassed and alarmed her. She had been serenely unconscious of his masculinity, and now he forced it upon her notice. His hands were in his trouser pockets when he spoke to her, his eyes narrowing and then widening as if to hypnotise her. And against her will she was slowly hypnotised.

When the long hot day was over and they sat on the terrace in deck-chairs Ugo's face seemed all aglow towards her, pale under the sunburned cheeks, his whole body trembling. 'Please do not let me spend another night alone,' he implored her. Staggering forward from the shadows, he leaned over her with ravenous lips. Spontaneously her bare arms drew his face down to hers and it was a repetition of the old, old story. The pressure of Ugo's lips opened a hidden crater of bubbling lava. Ugo took advantage of the eruption to undress Flora with frantic fingers, and Flora, half-swooning, submitted to his volcanic embraces. He transmitted his juvenile ardour to her languid limbs, and the flow of his pent-up emotion was like the moon that turns the tides. Proud of shattering her prudent reserve, Ugo became exuberantly cheerful. He laughed and sang and recovered his hearty appetite. 'Parlami d'amore, Mariù,' he sang operatically.

Flora had felt she was humouring a sick child but she

could not deny that the experience had been pleasurable. It was an age since her senses had been so voluptuously stirred, but it was a matter of the senses merely – her mind scarcely entered into it. This was so distinct from her desire for Elmer that her conscience was clear. She could see no harm in her response to the poor boy's craving – on the contrary. Something of the kind was bound to happen sooner or later, she reflected, and it might have happened sooner considering the unsuspected flame of Ugo's temperament. It was flattering to be adored by a creature so much younger, but she did not intend to let him renew the bombardment.

She had not reckoned with his stubborn will. Having tasted honey, he was gluttonous for more. Flora made excuses, feigned indisposition. 'Be a good boy. There is a season for everything. Run away and leave me alone!'

But he slipped off his clothes and paid no attention to her feeble protests. Gripping and enfolding her in his brawny arms, he hugged her to his hairy chest until, panting and gasping, she gave up the unequal struggle. He sucked her nipples and nibbled her armpits. 'Stop it, you little tiger!' she cried. But he only stopped her mouth with his own while massaging her mound of Venus. 'You are all mine!' he whispered triumphantly.

'Gently, gently. You hurt!'

'I want to wound you with love.' He who had seemed so wan and listless was insatiable. 'Love me with your lips, your tongue, your teeth,' he pleaded.

'Enough is enough. Let me sleep!' she replied wearily, pushing him off the pillow. He soon dozed off after his strenuous exertions, to renew them after dawn.

How absurd it was really, she mused, and how undignified. Flora was annoyed with herself for letting compassion get the better of her. She must be more severe with Ugo in future. That the young were seduced by their elders struck her as a popular fallacy, for she had had no intention of being seduced by this boy. But he was indomitably persistent. If she complained of a headache, he said, 'Let me kiss it away!' And his kisses were invariably a prelude to more substantial endearments.

She persuaded Ersilia, her maid, to move into the next bedroom as a chaperon. Ersilia resented Ugo's appropriation of her *Signora*. She called him *lo zoppo* and repeated the proverb 'chi va con lo zoppo impara a zoppicare', which could be paraphrased as 'Bad company contaminates the good'. However, as she slept like a log she never heard Ugo's nocturnal forays into the Signora's bed or the crescendo of vibrations that ensued. She pretended not to know how far he had gone with her.

He could hardly have gone much farther. Despite her resolutions Flora frequently succumbed to his blandishments. She saw him as the incarnation of a pagan satyr, and he made her feel pagan, too, with his musky smell and his primitive cries of ecstasy, at first sipping, then gulping her like a beaker of heady wine, pouring his wild essence through her veins until she sank back with the moan of a ravished nymph. A dreamless sleep followed with Ugo's tousled head on her bosom. He was still there when Ersilia came with coffee in the morning. Ersilia was startled. 'For shame!' she shouted. 'Cover yourself decently and go back to your own room.'

'I'm quite comfortable here, thank you. And why should I cover the best part of me? At least it does not limp. Now bring me an extra cup and a plate of peaches.'

'I only accept commands from the Signora.'

Flora quietly ordered another cup for Ugo as if it were nothing out of the ordinary.

'He will have to fetch it himself. This is scandalous. I'm leaving. I have my reputation to consider. The neighbours will gossip.'

'Let everybody mind his own business. Why shouldn't Ugo share my bed? Stop fussing.'

Ersilia was so fond of the Signora that after perfunctory grumbling she changed her mind when Flora raised her wages. After all, the Signora was a foreigner with an exotic outlook. Though she never went to Mass, she was generous to the poor. Nobody ever appealed to her in vain. She had helped Ersilia's family and paid for her old mother's kidney operation. So she stayed on, smothering her indignation with the lame interloper.

The scene with Ersilia cleared the air between them. Flora appeared less often with Ugo in public, on the beach or at cocktail parties. By day he was studious and retiring, but by night he was the same predatory lover.

'Where's Ugo?' a neighbour might ask out of casual curiosity.

'How should I know? Busy working, I expect. I seldom see him nowadays. . . .'

'What sort of work?'

'He paints and writes poetry.'

The subject was dropped since her neighbours were interested in neither. 'Flora has always specialised in lame ducks,' as Ronald Lipson remarked.

Even in bed with Ugo it never crossed Flora's mind that she was being unfaithful to Elmer. Elmer was on a higher plane, more spiritual than physical, and on this lofty summit she was faithful to him in thought, if not in deed. At the back of her mind she was always conscious of this special affinity. Though they had never lived together, she knew him through and through: he was a solid rock of friendship as well as an ideal mate.

In spite of her association with Ugo she could not take him seriously as a male. With his sobs and sighs and gushes of emotion he was subconsciously feminine: his masculinity was superficial; it could not penetrate her deepest core. She had never spoken to him about Elmer.

While dreaming Ugo had called her *Mamma*, which revealed that he regarded her as a mother as well as a mistress, and she felt a mother's responsibility towards him. Now he wanted her in the daytime as well as at night, and he wept when she refused, however kindly. His demands had become oppressive, a sort of moral blackmail. There was something diseased about his turbulent lust: he was becoming vicious. Instead of soothing her senses he exasperated them, reminding her ironically of those sex machines on sale in Scandinavia, reducing her to an object of evacuation. She felt numb when she was not hostile, and as indifferent to his embraces as to those of the divorced husband who had only made love to her when he was drunk.

Mortified by her apathy, Ugo persevered in futile efforts to stimulate her till Flora burst out laughing.

Swiftly he drew away from her, offended and bewildered.

'Why do you laugh?' he asked her.

'If you could see yourself, you would laugh, too. You are such an acrobat. Isn't it rather tiring? Wouldn't it be better to go swimming in the sea?'

Ugo fell silent. He watched her in dismay, for he had little sense of humour where sex was concerned. He had been intensely serious, and proud of his conquest. 'So you do not love me!' he gasped.

'Did I ever say that I loved you? I feel affection for you but that is different. I could not bear to see you unhappy, and you looked so miserable.'

'I am much more miserable now.'

It was blackmail, sheer blackmail. He threatened suicide and cut his wrists to prove that he was in earnest. Again Flora had to play the role of comforter, and he would not be comforted without her physical surrender. He loosened his bandages and bled copiously over her blouse. Ersilia screamed at the sight of it and wanted to call a doctor. 'Questo zoppo ci porta la iella,' she exclaimed. 'This lame one brings us bad luck.' But the cuts were not deep, and Flora bandaged them while Ersilia praised her pluck. Shaking a finger at Ugo, she shrilled: 'Stop frightening us. This is no way for a guest to behave. And the poor Signora has treated you with such kindness. Try to be more considerate in future.'

Ugo calmed down when they returned to the apartment in Florence. He took up his painting again, and Flora posed for him – but not, as he wished, in the nude. The result was admired by her friends. Undoubtedly he showed promise, they agreed; he could catch a certain likeness. Flora persuaded others to pose for him with the prospect of holding an exhibition.

At last the longed-for telegram arrived. Elmer asked Flora to join him in New York. His wife having 'passed away' he was free to remarry. Flora rushed out to buy her ticket and started packing. Ugo was banished from her mind; of course, she would provide for him and he could stay on in the apartment for the time being. Ersilia would remain in charge. Flora's friends were invited to an impromptu farewell party.

When Ugo returned from the studio Ronald was playing 'The Man I Love' on the drawing-room piano and the canasta-players were toasting Flora and wishing her a happy voyage. Everybody was kissing her and cracking jokes about wedding bells. Flora stood flushed and radiant in their midst. Ugo peered at the festive gathering with haggard eyes, invisible to the crowd of merrymakers. He had been surprised to notice a couple of suitcases beside the front entrance. 'What does it mean?' he asked Ersilia.

'Haven't you heard?' she replied with a sly grin. 'The Signora is going home to be married.'

'Impossible!' he cried. 'This cannot be true. She has told me nothing about it.'

'Her friends in the drawing-room are celebrating the glad news. Her essential bags are packed; she leaves tomorrow by the night train to Paris.'

Reeling under the shock, Ugo had an impulse to shout: 'She's my woman. She belongs to me!' But he spun round and fled, his brain in a chaotic whirl. His whole horizon had collapsed as in an earthquake. 'She's going and soon she will be gone,' he muttered, 'and what will become of me now?' He was appalled by Flora's deception: everything he had thought safe in the world came crashing down. He had no other friend in the world, nor any next of kin. She had picked him up and dropped him like a soiled handkerchief. The woman was heartless, but he would not allow her to desert him so easily. He wandered through the streets in a trance of despair. How could he stop her? It occurred to him that perhaps Ersilia had invented the whole thing just to spite him. Yes, that was plausible since she had always hated him.

Half-gliding, half-hopping with nervous apprehension he made his way back to the apartment for an explanation. Ersilia need not announce him for he had the keys. He found Flora resting in her bedroom after the party, her eyes blindfold as usual against the light. Ugo was dazed by the beautiful curves of her body as if he had never seen it before. He knelt beside her and deliriously kissed her hands.

'So you have come,' she said. 'I was wondering where you had gone. We missed you at my farewell party.'

'Farewell for whom?'

'I have been recalled to New York by my fiancé. At last we are free to marry.'

So it was true. All that Ugo had been prepared to say stuck in the throat. He gazed at her piteously like a beaten dog, his pallor alarmingly bloodless.'Why did you not warn me?' he wailed. 'Have I proved unworthy of your confidence?'

'I did not want to hurt your feelings. You are so terribly sensitive. The fact is I was engaged even before we met, but my fiancé was tied to another woman. It was an impossible situation and I had no desire to discuss it with you or with anyone else. What did you ever know about my real self?'

'I knew you as a woman. You made a man of me. Does that mean nothing to you, nothing at all?'

'It is nothing beside my engagement to a man of my own age and nationality.'

'You have played with me like a puppet, and now what am I to do? You have been everything to me. How can I exist without you?'

'Don't be melodramatic. I shan't be gone indefinitely – and of course we'll keep in touch. You might even come to America, but it is too early to decide. Ersilia can look after you in the meantime, and I'll give you the money for living expenses if that's what is worrying you. We must be practical and realistic, *non è vero*?'

'So you only gave yourself to me out of pity. Have you told your fiancé about that or would you prefer me to tell him? It would make a pretty story, ''The American Beauty and the Crippled Pauper'', to read on your honeymoon.'

'Yes, Ugo, I pitied you sincerely with all my heart. But you pitied yourself much more. I had hoped to cure you of it as you were cured of polio, but I see that I have failed. Your self-pity is self-destructive, your lameness has gone to your head. You insisted on being loved when you only loved yourself. You needed someone to whom you could hitch your ego and I was that unlucky person. You repay me with bitter insolence. I can leave you without regret.'

'You cannot deny that you enjoyed our nights together. Your American fiancé will make you miss them.'

She gave him a resounding slap. 'Get out of my sight. Fuori!'

He spat at her: 'Sporca puttana!

He tried to climb on top of her and there was a furious struggle. Flora rang for Ersilia but there was no answer, for she had sent her on some final errands. 'Puttana, puttana!' he hissed. But Flora was the stronger and she sent him flying. 'Storpio maligno! Via!'

Cursing her, he tottered out of the bedroom where he had made love to her so often. If only he had a revolver! He must make do with a substitute. In the kitchen he chose the sharpest knife he could find and hid it under his jacket.

'Back again! This is insufferable. Once and for all go away, or I'll call the *carabinieri*!'

'Addio!' he muttered, and plunged the knife between her breasts. To make doubly certain he withdrew it and thrust it violently into her belly and thighs, drenching the sheets in blood, then wiping the blade on her hair. He had intended to cut his throat, but it seemed too messy, so he replaced the knife in the kitchen and threw himself out of the window.

It looked as if all the lilies of Florence, male, female and strictly botanical, had assembled for Flora's funeral in the Episcopalian church. The massed tuberoses round the coffin were more overpowering than fumes of incense. All Flora's friends and many who had scarcely known her filled the pews with streaming eyes and drawn expressions. Their sobs and sniffles were muted by the organ where Ronald Lipson, who had fortified himself with gin, played 'I'll See You Again' as a voluntary while the congregation waited for the coffin to be carried up the aisle. The coffin was surprisingly small, as if Flora had shrunk from loss of blood. Ersilia wept hysterically and had to be supported when, swaying to her knees, she placed a bouquet of immortelles on the shiny lid of the coffin. Having taken an extra swig of gin from his hip-flask, a relic of Prohibition days, Ronnie played 'The Man I Love' *pianissimo*, in lieu of a hymn. Nobody thought of poor Elmer, who was expecting Flora in New York. In any case, he would have been a stranger.

The officiating clergyman paid eloquent tribute to Flora's philanthropic heart and democratic spirit. She had done her utmost to comfort and alleviate the distressed. It was no exaggeration to assert that she had fallen a victim to her boundless charity. An angel on earth, she had joined the angels in Heaven, a shining example to all of us. Though her charity began at home, she never let it stay there. When her care for the handicapped was mentioned some were reminded of Ugo, her last lame duck.

'I always mistrusted him', said Ronnie. 'To my mind, he was a warning against indiscriminate charity, whatever the parson may say.'

The owner of Flora's apartment on the Arno was afraid that nobody would want to rent it after the sensational murder, but he was mistaken. He was flooded with requests to visit it, and Flora's bedroom in particular. He told me that he had been offered considerable sums by fetishists for the bloodstained sheets. Unfortunately the sheets had gone to the laundry, but Ersilia sold the kitchen knife for the price of a brand-new radio.

Safe Wintering

Terence Wheeler

I work down in Falmouth now but the other weekend I travelled over home to Rothesey, and a dastard old bit of coast she is, by Christ if she in't, what with the marshes and the snow and that damn old north-easterly you know won't give over till March. When I was at sea I was with a firm in Chicago plying the Lakes and they called that windy. Blast, I say they don't know what windy is compared to Rothesey. And she's that flat they did used to say it only want somebody to get a boil on their neck and they mark it on the charts for a hazard to navigation. The ground shelves so gradual that the sea goes out half a mile at low water and then there's just shingle and hard mud, those mats of brown grass and the stumps of the old fish-weirs from years back. At high water there's no depth for a vessel with any draught to speak of, except for the harbour channel, and when that dastard wind comes across the marshes she take your legs off and any other bits you're not hanging on tight to.

The town sit along the shore, all slate and yellow brick with a handful of timber places mostly white. She's always been poverty-stricken and so she look, like a body who's been hard done by all their life. And no surprise, for I know for a certain fact there are people in the town with drawerfuls of dud cheques from before the war from theatre people who used to come down to do their tomcatting on the quiet. They was supposed to come for the sake of the lobsters. You can imagine, big plump white lobsters with feathers on and button boots more like. Any lobsters they come for they brought with them, our old lady used to say.

No surprise the people are suspicious still. The Queen's

Hotel have got a IOU from Sir Henry Irving written in Guinness, and he never been back to my knowledge. The fishermen won't look at anything but cash money. They say they don't go out just to make free for nothing presents to crackjaw Londoners. They've got too many widows for that. And half the fishermen can't swim, because if you're in seaboots it don't make no odds either way.

Last winter a skipper called Darrant drowned right in the harbour and his mate nearly, trying to get him out. His widow opened a wool-shop when she sold the boat. Her father was a Bates and he was a artist. Years ago he objected when the council wanted to put in main drainage, and on the Monday morning they come back and he was laying in the trench in a coffin with his easel and a case of brandy. It took him all week to drink it and then he got up and went indoors and had a bath. He said it needed a real man to know when he was beat. This Mrs Darrant had a brother called Alec who was in demolition, but everybody called him 'the Animal'. He was the one whose wife got turned out of the Ketch and he come along in the night and tipped a lorryload of rubble through the plate glass, and when the police went round to his yard they look at his tax disc and it was made of Green Shield stamps. This Mrs Darrant has only got one leg, and the tale is that when she was a girl they sent her away to a boarding school and she jump out of the dormitory window. They were all divers on her mother's side, the Hatchards.

I'd go back tomorrow if there was work there. Both our families are there, but my wife could get a job sooner than me and I won't stand for that. She won't let me go back to sea and I don't argue. I've been on that National Assistance and I don't relish it.

When the train leaves Bleassatt the last stretch to Rothesey is over the marshes and there is nothing for company but dykes, sheep and pylons and the North Sea is off out of sight until, about a mile before the town, it suddenly reaches in beside the embankment and at high water you would think you were riding on it.

I stood in the corridor with the window down and when we slowed for the level crossing I could hear the reeds beside the line and a boat's rigging clattering against the mast, which carries a long way. It was late afternoon and there was a mist and the sun was dark on the snow. We passed Jonathan Pinel's place on its own on the beach. A curtain was flapping through a broken window and the workshop door was gone, and I thought: Blast and bugger, at least somebody could have come out and do enough to keep the vandals off of it. And, as we were passing, a old dog fox come out of the workshop and look at the train and I thought: Blast, don't that tell it all; even the brutes know he isn't coming back. Bugger, I could've weep and that's swearing to it.

In the Ketch that night there was Uncle Payne and Uncle Joseph and Joseph's son Dwaine, and Banjo Hatchard, myself, and the landlord. The plank walls were sweating and the marble tables running with steam, and the bar was filling up with smoke, which I can't abide any more than I can abide listening to old men tell old lies.

'What're you going to eat, Payne?' Joseph says.

'I'll have a bit of cheese and a half-onion.'

'What about our chillyconcarney?' asks the landlord.

'Blast, what're you doing that old muck for?'

'He'd do turd on toast if anybody asked for it, wouldn't you?' says Joseph.

'I'd have to send out for it.'

'How's that?'

'I don't keep it on the premises.'

'Funny, I heard you did, heh, heh, heh!' says Payne.

So I got out. Other people's smoke and other people's dirty talk, I can't be doing with either, not for any price.

'Uncle Payne, I'm lending your stick,' I said.

'You have her back by closing or I shan't get home.'

'Be doing a decent woman a good turn, wouldn't I?'

'Bugger, I do you a good turn, boy, I bend your jaw!' he says.

I walked to the harbour gates down along and I stopped outside the bakery to see them baking for Saturday and take the smell of it, then I turned west upon the sea-wall with ice underfoot and the sea on my right hand. We used to come there for driftwood with a handcart, the two of us, and fetch it back to Tin House.

The Pinels were sailmakers, and Jonathan's father had a loft in Upper Wall. He was a lovely man and always up to something new. He had a smack called *Quadrille*. In the summer he and Jonathan took a Punch and Judy show round the markets. When *Quadrille* got driven ashore he broke her up and used her timbers to build them a place on the beach. It was roofed with corrugated iron, so they called it Tin House. You have never seen two chaps more lord and master than they were in that house. They got away with murder, so it looked to me coming from our house to theirs. Mrs Pinel worshipped the very mud on their boots. She was a small happy woman with olive skin and her hair always in a bun on top of her head, and Mr Pinel would hang about the scullery waiting for his meal, getting under her feet and touching her up when he got her in the larder. She never minded. You could have sworn she liked it.

She died when Jonathan was thirteen, and his father's sister came to keep house, and she damn soon clipped their wings for the both of them. She was a big woman with stiff sandy hair and an overall lashed round her middle, and after she came life was penal servitude for Jonathan till he went to sea. He was never much of a talker but the worst of what he did have to say he kept for her. We took our dinghy up Bleassatt Creek one time and we were laying under the stars and he told me flat if he ever got away from Rothesey they would have to bring him back in a box. When he did go he never so much as said goodbye to her, he had that much feeling against her.

He was made for the Navy. He even looked like a matelot – narrow shoulders and no chest or hips, like a yard of drainpipe in blue flannel. His hair was so white that his eyebrows and lashes were near-invisible, but he was handy with any kind of work you put him to and sure of himself. The maths teacher called him one of Mother Nature's born petty officers and it was true.

The year after he went into the service, I went to sea myself and didn't lay eyes on him for years. Then one evening Uncle Payne came in for his supper. I was married to Anne by then and had come ashore, I thought, for good and we were living with my mother in Shamrock Street. Jonathan's father had died years before and the aunt had gone back to wherever she came from, somewhere the other side of Bleassatt.

'Your mate's home. He's got hisself wed.'

He had met her in Singapore. I saw her real Chinese name on a letter once, but he called her Jade. Her family had bought him out of the Navy and he had lived with them for several years. She had a brother with a business in London. They had set up in Tin House with the first child, though she would not send him to school. She taught him at home.

The first time I saw her was in Upper Wall. It was summer and she had come in shopping. She always wore Chinese costume in warm weather, some kind of silky flowered shirt and trousers of the same, and her hair on top of her head and fixed with a comb. People were staring, but if she noticed she did not show it. I can't remember ever seeing her speak to anyone in the street. In winter she used to put on clothes of his and a balaclava helmet, and her bun used to push up at the top. Even then I thought it was a shame and wondered why she made such a scarecrow of herself. I asked Anne, but she said nothing you could make sense of.

The first time I saw Jonathan again was at the harbour. He was too busy to talk for long even if he had wanted to, which he didn't. He had bought a derelict smack up at Lowestoft and was seeing her towed in.

'Hello, mate,' I said. We were in our thirties by then, but there was no mistaking him.

'Hello, Gordon.'

'Yours?'

'That's right.' There was a surliness about him as if no matter what you said to him he would take it the wrong way, and as time went on I realised it was permanent.

'*Quadrille*,' I read on her stern.

'That's right.'

'What're you doing with yourself?'

'A bit of woodworking, a bit of pottery.'

'You ought to come round some time.'

'I'll ask her,' he said, moving off.

'Nice to see you back,' I called.

'No choice of mine,' he said over his shoulder.

Winter came on and they had another baby. I would see Jade in the street in her dusty greatcoat and riding an old black delivery-bike with the baby and shopping in the carrier. It should have been comical, but she was so upright and inside herself it would have been a sin to stare.

Then one day we got talking at the bakery. I don't know how she knew me, but she went on for a long time about how seldom she could afford to buy shop bread. It surprised me how anybody so dignified could demean herself and her husband like that. After all, it reflects on the man more than on the wife. She was a very refined person and spoke beautiful English and must have had a good education. She asked what the Rothesey Theatre Group were putting on, and I said *Antony and Cleopatra*, not that I knew but I could see the poster across the street.

They came round next evening. I went to the door and there he was in a suit and tie and her in her Chinese clothes with a little painted vase full of sweets. When she came into our passage her scent was heavy and musky. They had brought a bottle of brandy and we sat in our back room for the best part of three hours. She tried to talk about politics and books, but we must have disappointed her because after a while she stopped talking and it was plain she was not listening.

Jonathan told us about her grandmother who went to the

States from Ireland as a nursemaid and met Jade's grandfather in a park and went back to China with him.

Afterwards Anne and my mother went into ecstasies
about that tale and how romantic it was, but Anne was not
smitten with Jade herself. She said you could see where
Jade got her temper from. I couldn't see that she had a
temper – the very opposite, I thought. And if she did talk
too much about money she had good reason because he was
not in regular work. It seemed that when he was out East he
had heard about some long-lost red glaze and the first thing
he did when he came back was to build a kiln. Every month
her family sent him a package of joss ash, which he thought
was the secret. Jade used to laugh about it and say he was
making their fortune, but Anne said that Jade no more
believed it than pigs flying. All the same Jonathan set a lot of
store by it, that and the boat.

All in all it was a mystification to me what had possessed
him to come back, seeing how he felt about the place. Then
one day he let drop that the Chinese, once they give you
anything, want to own you body and soul. I took it to mean
her family.

A couple of years passed and he was getting on very
slowly with *Quadrille*. Her timbers were farther gone that he
had thought and she would have kept a dozen men in work,
he said. He kept her at a jetty below Tin House. All he could
use was stuff he got cheap from the yards, but it was beyond
me where the cash was coming from until I went over there
one day. We went down to take a look at her.

'What're you going to do when she's finished?' I said.

'Wander about. Chartering maybe. Go back East.'

Anne thought he had a notion of sailing her back to Jade's
family in triumph, his own boat and the secret of that glaze,
but by then he had as good as given up the glaze and was
giving all his time to *Quadrille*.

'Tell me to take a funny walk if you want, but where's the
money coming from?' I said.

'In here,' he said and took me into the workshop.

Jade was sitting at a bench stacked with little bits of

Chinese crockery, vases and dishes and so on. Her brother used to send them down by the crateful, and she painted on the designs.

But, blast, it was cold in there. They had one of those industrial blower heaters in the doorway, but it was off.

'Why haven't you got that on?' he shouted at her.

'I don't need it,' she shrugged.

'I've told you before, you keep that bugger on.'

She just pursed her mouth.

'You work better when you're warm,' I said.

She looked up and gave me a polite little smile, very polite, very resigned.

'My work is excellent,' she said.

'I didn't mean that,' I apologised. She had the knack of making you feel apologetic and afterwards not having a clue why.

She was wearing the same old coat and trousers and on her hands some thin flowery gloves with the fingers cut off to make mittens, but when I looked at what she was doing it was the most delicate, sweetly pretty thing you have seen in your life. But it was so slow. There and then I said to myself: It won't do, my gel, where's the profit? They weren't even working for themselves, for it all went back to her brother to sell.

But, to give them their due, to my mind nobody on God's earth worked harder than them during those years.

I was taking any work I could find. Some days I went over and cut logs for their stove, which was the same old iron contraption that his father put in. In the house everything was changed round since his aunt's time. It would be hot, and there was always a mess of spars and tackle about the living-room, but here and there Jade had cleared herself a space for her ornaments and bits of furniture she had brought over with her, like tiny islands of her in the middle of an ocean of him. The children were well fed. She taught them to read in English and Chinese. She was never still two minutes together, but he would sit silent at the table for his food while she hummed away to herself at the log-stove. Have you ever had the feeling a show is being put on for

your benefit but cannot make out what it is you are supposed to be noticing? Sometimes, if it had not been for the
gloominess, you could have sworn it was his mother about
the place. A glimpse out of the corner of your eye, the skin
and the hair and her slenderness.

'Gordon,' she started sweetly one day, 'what kind of
cooker does Anne prefer?'

'I don't rightly know.'

'Gas or electricity?'

'Our old lady's got gas. I think.'

'Ah,' she sighs. 'At home we have all electricity. Thank
you so much for the wood.'

'That's all right.' What else was I supposed to say?

'It is a most great kindness.'

'Glad to do it,' I said. Blast, I was being paid to do it. But I
knew it was not me she was talking to. And when the food
came there wasn't more than a morsel of it you could bring
yourself to stomach.

One thing that struck me was he never seemed to touch
her, not even to get her attention or help her, not even a
hand on the elbow. I don't remember why he brought it up,
but he said to me once: 'They can't abide to be touched,
Orientals. We were told that before we went abroad. You
must never lay a finger on them, Orientals.'

'She's your wife.'

'That doesn't mean I'm not to respect her. When she
wants me to touch her she's got her own way of telling me.'

When I told Anne she said: 'I bet that's not often.'

'How do you mean?'

'I mean what I say.'

'No, bugger my gel, what do you mean?'

'Think about it, you great lump. Do I have to do everything for you?'

Once when we were all of us out on the marshes for a
walk, Jade got down a dyke after a flower and reached up
her hand for him to help her. He looked as if he had been
paid the biggest honour known to man, but she gave him no
smile.

'He's afraid of her,' Anne said later.

'He must be fond of her.'

'Maybe, but he's afraid of her more. And he depends on her. He doesn't like that.'

'She worships him,' I said. 'They do, these Eastern women. They're brought up to.'

'I expect that's what he thought. Goes to show, doesn't it? She never wanted to come here and he's being made to pay for it.' She started brushing the sofa.

'I don't see it.'

'No, you wouldn't. She's got a will of iron, that one. Come on, shift your carcass, I'm dusting there.'

Once when I was over at Tin House, Jade and I were alone. I had been out of work for eight or nine months on the trot and had a chance of going back to sea. One voyage would clear off what we owed, and half a dozen trips could get us the deposit on a place of our own, but Anne would not hear of it. Her philosophy was we could put up with anything so long as we were together.

'But of course you must go,' Jade said. 'The husband must do what is expected. Money is necessary. It buys what the body requires and also the mind. We are mistaken if we think it will not bring happiness. Without it there is no happiness. Not to understand this and not to act accordingly is only to lay up misery.'

So I signed on without telling Anne. Jesus wept, there was old hell in our place that night. I'll never go through days like that again, not if I have any say.

That trip was supposed to be four months but it turned into seven. Never again, not in this life.

Six or so years after they came to Rothesey, Jade left him. They agreed for the children to go to her brother and she went home to her family. I walked over there one of my first evenings ashore. He was burning her things out on the mud. The sparks flew into the night sky and the fire shone in the pools left by the tide.

'Do you want a drink?' I said.

'I don't mind.'

We went below to the cabin of *Quadrille* where he was living. He talked about the future, selling the house to finish the boat and having the children back with him, but I couldn't see him raising the kind of money he needed. No more could he, if the truth be told.

'You could strike lucky,' I said.

'How long have you been a comedian?' he said.

'Go back to sea?'

'Sod that for a lark. I had enough of that from her, the cow.'

We finished the bottle and I went home.

'He's very very low,' I said to Anne.

'He'll float; he's the type,' she said.

He went through a few casual jobs, then started up on his own. I saw him going about the town with his tools on the front of the bike – gardening and house repairs and so on.

Anne and I used to go to school with the Goldfinch girls, Molly and Maureen. Their father was Goldfinch the newsagent. He was widowed when they were little. He sent them both to college to be teachers. They were large girls with sallow skin and reddish hair, and they both seemed to go in for small men when they were young. They didn't exactly look like horses, but people used to say if you wanted to tell them apart the best way was to look at the jockey. Maureen emigrated as soon as she could. Molly was an art teacher and kept house for her father.

When old Goldfinch died Molly was left alone in the house. She gave up teaching and sold the business, though Anne advised her not to. The only times she went out were to slip along to the shops and go to church. I would see her sometimes in her pink woolly beret and a great tweed cloak. Not walking: she didn't walk, she cantered. And other times she would be staring for minutes on end in the window of an empty shop, not looking at herself but killing time rather than go back to the house on her own. When she talked to you, if she talked to you, she was twittery and spoke with a silly little-girl voice and wrung her hands without knowing she was. A couple of minutes in her company and you would be all of a jump. But Anne said anybody would be twittery if they had had a lifetime of running after old Goldfinch's every whim and fancy, for he was an old swine if ever there was one. All the same she was the most unappetising piece of female I ever laid eyes on.

Anne used to go round there once or twice a week. Molly liked having the children, and it made a change for Anne from the Baptist Young Wives.

One day she came home and said: 'Jonathan was there today, doing the garden.'

'He's got a job for life.'

'He's going to do the roof next.'

'That won't make his fortune,' I said.

'Won't it?' she said.

And pretty soon it was plain that, instead of him finding himself jobs to do there, Molly was inventing them for him. Then in October she moved into Tin House with him.

'Never!' I said.

'She's letting her place,' Anne said. And, blast, she was pleased with herself.

I tried to picture Jonathan and Molly in the same house together.

'Well,' I said, 'if they see each other through the winter they'll be doing well. Personally, I'd just as soon winter with a crate of mackerel.'

'Is that the best you can say?'

'What do you want me to say?'

'I see,' she says, and when she went into the scullery she near took the door off the hinges.

It was about this time that Rothesey got in on the fake nautical furniture racket, boxes painted up to look like sea-chests with coils of rope and ship portraits on the lids and the names of imaginary skippers. They would pick up an old chest, trim it with brass corners artificially tarnished and paint it up with *Capt. U. Phart, H.M.S. Cantankerous, 1803* and the picture of some square-rigger out of a book. Any fool knows that with a real sea-chest the picture goes on the inside of the lid, but they were shipping hundreds of them to the Continent and the States.

It was a month before Anne could drag me over to Tin House. Molly was radiant, and he was putting on flesh. The women stayed inside while he took me out to the work-shop. Down one side was a stack of these chests with first coats on them, then round the other walls he had built long benches where there were more being decorated.

'It's a bloody production line,' I said. 'How much do you get for these?'

'Some forty quid, some sixty.'

'She's artistic,' I said when I had started to get over it.

'She's quick,' he grudged as if it could have choked him.

There was a new van under the lean-to.

Molly was a new person; none of that twittering and pretending she was a little girl. The house was warm and pretty, and when we sat down to dinner there were little flowered menus on the table to tell us we were getting *Potage Madrilène* and *Chicken Véronique*. She showed us the desk where she ran the accounts, and when we left they were standing on the sea-wall hand in hand.

'He's making a bleeding convenience of her,' I said.

'Well, she looks well on it.'

'He's having her on!' I said.

'I don't see that. They're both grown up and she's better off than on her own, twiddling her thumbs and going off her head.' Anne looked sideways at me, slyly. 'And if they see each other through the winter, they'll be doing well.'

I stumped on, a few paces ahead of her.

'Do they sleep in the same bed?'

'I expect so,' she said.

'I think it's wicked.'

'Do you?'

'And she's got him a van,' I said. 'Bugger and blast, if you was to hang that chap from the ceiling, he'd fall on his feet!'

I ran into them coming out of Underwood's, the men's

outfitters, one morning. He was carrying a parcel and she was putting her chequebook away.

'Good morning, Gordon,' she says sweetly, 'and how are you?'

'Mustn't grumble,' I lied.

'What're you doing?' he says.

'Nothing. Looking for work.'

'How very fortunate,' she says. 'We need someone, don't we, darling?'

If I hadn't needed it so bad, I would have told them what to do with it. Him, I mean, because I had nothing against her. At least it was good to have a reason to get up in the mornings. At five I used to get their bread from the bakery before the shop opened, and that was a pleasure in itself, then I cycled along the sea-wall to Tin House. If the tide was right, there would be dunlin out on the mud and the early sun picking out the silver on a flight of geese trailing back to the marshes. I opened up the workshop, mixed some paint, sharpened the tools and laid them out, and then went in for breakfast with them.

She used to sing about the kitchen and be primping herself ready for his lordship to appear, and I thought as I watched her: Well, missus, you're getting your money-worth if it's no more than in bed – for I was certain sure she must have been a virgin till then.

He would come out at last and fetch her a whack on the rump.

'Come on, you cow, shift yourself!'

'For you?' she'd laugh.

'Who else'd have you?'

So she would laugh again, and I was pleased for her sake. And for my own. Long might it last. At least I had wages. But he needn't think I was fooled by his capers.

One time in the workshop I was just outside and they were busy. He started singing one of his father's songs.

> 'Did you ever see a wild goose
> Winging o'er the ocean?

They're just like those pretty girls
With their rigging all in motion.
Ranzle, ranzle, weigh!'

He came behind her and touched her bosom and kissed her ear, and she reached up and stroked his cheek. Blast, if I couldn't have gone and tell her there and then what he was about, but where would it have got me?

'That woman's a fool,' I said to Anne.

'I expect so. Still, if they see each other through the winter. . . .'

And so it went on, them coining money and me not taking home a fraction of what they were making in a week, and we were into December.

But then one day I had to go looking for him for his dinner. He was sitting on the beach spreading out a bundle of ship's papers which had been washed up.

> *MANIFIESTA DE CARGA*
> *Clase y Nombre de Buque: motonave 'CIUDAD DE GUAYAQUIL'*
> *Nacionalidad: ecuatoriana*
> *Nombre del Capitán: H. Munoz*
> *Puerto de Emisión: Bremen*
> *Destino Final: Guayaquil/Ecuador*

'Spanish,' I said.

'Ecuador', he said.

We did not see him for the rest of the day, and next morning he started working on *Quadrille* again.

With him full-time on the boat, Molly and I had to manage on our own. She missed him in the workshop but said nothing about it to me. All the same, they were a lot quieter together.

Then one day she came home and put a stack of books on the table about navigation and cooking at sea and so on.

'What's this?' he said.

'I thought I'd treat myself for Christmas,' she said.

'That's nice,' he said and he went out without eating.

A few days before Christmas, I got there in the morning and the van was gone. She came out with the delivery-bike and hitched up her skirt.

'He's gone to get the children,' she called to me. 'I'm going shopping if I don't kill myself on this thing first!'

She fell off twice in the first ten yards but there was no dampening her spirits, she was so full of the joys of spring.

Whatever hopes she had, it wasn't to be. When the children came he kept them by him all the time and hardly let her do a thing for them, carping at her in front of them and contradicting her.

I said to Anne: 'Damn fine Christmas for little 'uns. Blast, if he didn't want it known he was living with a woman, why th' hell did he bring them in the first place?'

'I'm sure I can't say,' she said as if she had expected no different.

Then one afternoon I heard him shouting in the bedroom.

'You're not their mother!'

'I know that.'

'Well, don't get any ideas.'

'How could I?' she sobbed.

'*How could I? How could I?*' he imitated. 'Oh, couldn't you just, you bitch!'

That night I said to Anne: 'I give her two months at the outside.'

'I'll see what I think on Boxing Day,' she said.

It was a hard winter on this coast. The sea froze and we got two feet of snow in a single night. The roads and the sea-wall were impossible so we had to go to Tin House along the beach, dragging the pushchairs over the stones and lugging them over the groynes every few yards. By

God, that was a game. But when we got indoors they had a tree and decorations and table covered with food and crackers. And after tea Jonathan brought out his father's Punch and Judy, and he and Molly gave us a show.

Things were going so well that I didn't know what time it was, but all of a sudden he disappeared into the children's bedroom and came out with their suitcases. At first I couldn't grasp what he was on about, but I said it to Anne then and I say it still: it were a wicked cruel thing to do to her.

'What are those for, Jonathan?' she said.

'Early start tomorrow,' he said without looking at her or us.

'Why?' she said.

'You know why.'

'But why *now*, why this minute?'

He said nothing but just took the cases and put them by the outside door.

'I asked you why *now*, Jonathan.' I never once saw her weep or lose her temper, but if she had been going to it would have been then.

He put on his coat and went out, and the children went on playing as if nothing had happened, which for them it hadn't.

'He wants them to see me at my worst,' she said to Anne. 'He wants them to see me scream and shout at him. I won't. They're fond of me, and I won't spoil it. When they go back they'll have good memories of me.'

When they left next morning she gave them packets of food for the journey and a kiss each, and they kissed her and called her Molly.

If I could have got other work I would have gone gladly. I didn't want to be round them, not to hear them or see them or have anything to do with it. Meal-times were a misery, so more often than not I took my own food and had it in the workshop. True, I had always expected it, but I never thought it would be like this. And she didn't deserve it, by

Christ she didn't. One day he would carry on as if she didn't exist, as if he could walk right through her. Another time he abused her, her work, her money, the way she looked, anything he could lay tongue to.

One morning he said to me: 'She's having a lay-in. You've been about the world, Gordon my boy, did you ever see a thing more hideous than a naked European woman in broad daylight? A big fat English female?'

She must have heard. He meant her to hear.

'You'll never find one with a better heart,' I said, but I could have just as soon hit him.

'Who does she remind you of?' he said.

'I don't know what you're on about.'

'My father's sister. Am I right?'

'Never,' I said.

'Well, bugger, you must be deaf and blind,' he said.

And so the weeks went on. I could always tell when things were worst because I would find her in front of the mirror snip-snipping away at her hair with nail-scissors. But the very worst days were when she got a letter from his children.

All the same, she was putting in eight or ten hours a day in the workshop while he was down on the boat or away at the yards. By the end of March he had done everything to *Quadrille* that he could do on his own and was waiting for her to be towed round to the harbour for the mast to be stepped. There were days when he did not get out of bed, and others when he got no farther than the stove and he spent his time watching Molly come in and out and waiting for a chance to hurt her. I had never seen him drink before.

The afternoon when the tug came for *Quadrille*, Molly and I stood on the beach to watch. I had no proof that Jonathan had been knocking her about and it was certain she was not going to tell me.

'I've never asked him for promises,' she said. 'I know I'm not their mother but I will go with them.'

'Of course you will; you've got a right,' I said, but I could have told her different.

Quadrille took ten or twelve days to rig, and then he brought her back. That night Molly took us out for a meal to celebrate. Jonathan did not speak the whole evening except to tell Anne he was going to London to fetch the children. As for Molly, she was pleasant and dignified and, I thought, a credit to herself to the last.

Next day he and I worked the morning without more than a word, and we were having dinner when he said: 'I know what you're thinking.'

'I don't give a sod for what you know nor you neither.'

'I'll have a good talk with her,' he said.

'You do that,' I said. 'That should put her straight, shouldn't it?' And I got up out of that cabin as quick as I could. I didn't want to breathe the same air with him even.

Just then the chance of the Falmouth job came up and a house along with it, and I was away a few days. When I came back I saw from the train that *Quadrille* was gone and a FOR SALE sign on the house.

When I got indoors Anne had a meal for me and our old lady was ironing in the scullery.

'Did you get it?' Anne asked.

'Yes.'

'Did you accept it?'

'Yes.'

'That's all right, then.'

She put my food in front of me with a sweet sweet smile. I could hear our old lady setting up a wail to herself in the coalhole. I thought to myself: This is one evening I go to the Ketch, by God!

'Jonathan's gone, then,' I said.

'Yes.'

'What's she doing with herself?'

'Gone with him, of course,' she said.

'Never!'

'She deserved to,' she said.

'Blast, gel, we don't always get what we deserve in this life, do we?'

'Yes, we do, every time,' she said.

Blast, that woman would drive a saint to the bottle, and that's swearing to it.

The Indian Girl

Giles Gordon

AT FIRST I didn't realise it was her hand.

The train was ludicrously overcrowded. It had been since, almost six hours previously, it left New Delhi station on its long journey to Amritsar – the holy city of the Sikhs with its fabulous Golden Temple – in the Punjab. Ludicrously overcrowded, that is, by the standards of Western travel, and of reasonable human safety.

If you haven't travelled on an Indian train, or only in the austere comfort of luxury air-conditioned or first-class carriages, it's hard to envisage how crammed they are. They make travel on the London Underground during the rush-hour seem like chauffeur-driven privacy. You think the carriages are full when the day begins but as it progresses and more and more people pile on you realise that, by Indian standards, they were almost empty. To start with, the trains are enormously long. You gather that as they slither and sidle into stations, like giant serpents or snakes, seeming to expend as little energy as is compatible with movement, trying to preserve what in the sullen heat of, say, April is left to them.

Each carriage is vast, too, like a rectangular barn. On the roof, tired fans bat round, apparently mocked by the heat so little effect do they have in dispelling the stagnant air. Three-quarters of the way across the carriage, lengthways, is a corridor or passage. On one side of it, against and beneath the windows, hard wooden slatted seats face each other, with space for one person on each seat. Above them are luggage-racks which are sufficiently deep and broad to accommodate a wealth of baggage, which is as well as on these trains there seems to be no other provision for luggage. On the other side of the corridor are rows of benches or seats facing each other, each seat again of hard slatted wood. There is no arm-rest or division between the individual places, or even an indication of how much space one person may not unreasonably be expected to occupy. In practice, four, five or six people – depending on width of bottom – sit on these benches, not to mention the passengers who crowd on to any spare edge of seat, and those who lean against the backs and sides of the places that adjoin the corridors.

The seats on this side of the carriage are surmounted by what might be thought of as luggage-racks but they're much lower from the roof than on the other side of the corridor, and indeed on Western trains. A baby elephant could perch there. They may be intended as luggage-racks but for nearly all the journey to Amritsar they were occupied by travellers, some sitting, some lying flat out and trying to sleep, others squatting down as Indians are liable to do in any circumstances. A Sikh on the rack above and opposite where I eventually obtained a perch began the journey in the crouching position but after a couple of hours had graduated to a fully stretched-out one and slept with the luggage, his own and that of others, both below him – a bedroll acted as pillow – and piled on top of him by later arrivals in the carriage as if he were inanimate. In trains as everywhere else, each Indian has to look after himself.

It was over an hour before I obtained a few inches of seat space. I managed it when a family dismounted at a small station and before everyone else standing in the vicinity of their seats had invaded the vacated bench. I was lucky to have been standing near. The seat I slipped into was at the end of the row, against the corridor. It was also the first row of seats in the carriage, close to the lavatory (the smell from which indicated its whereabouts) and the door.

The corridors, the whole length of the train, were crammed with passengers. It was quite impossible to go to the lavatories as people were sitting or standing in them with the doors forced open against the walls. There were so many people immediately outside them as well that progress could be made neither to nor from them. Had there been an accident to or on the train, the number of injured would surely have been colossal. It seemed, as a matter of course and convention, that women in saris – including grandmothers – sat or squatted on the floor whilst their menfolk, young and old, occupied seats when they could get them. Young mothers nursed their babies on the floor also, and people clambered over them all.

And yet in spite of this nightmarish impossible over-crowding – the stench of ordure and sweat and spiced food was overpowering almost from the beginning of the journey yet grew hugely as it continued – it didn't stop scores, hundreds of mainly young passengers at every stop (and they were frequent, at least one an hour) from leaping off the train to refill their water-bottles or cups or earthenware jars at station pumps. After a five- or ten-minute wait the engine would start moving, silently, no whistle or sound, as if trying to steal away unseen from the passengers who'd left the carriages. Those still without water would notice yet appear to take their time, fill their receptacles in turn and climb back up on to the moving train which by then might be beyond the end of the platform and out in the country-side. More often than not, they didn't even bother to slam shut the doors behind them.

Vendors of cold soft drinks (alcohol is forbidden altogether on Indian railways), Thermos flasks of hideously sweet but boiling tea, sharply spiced hot dishes, biscuits, sweetmeats, vegetables and fruit would somehow – ingeniously – thread their way, without too much apparent difficulty and without drenching people in food or drink, down the corridors, achieving quite a few sales. They would shout out in loud, raucous voices the nature of any commodity on offer, presumably in case those confronted with a particular delicacy failed to recognise it. They shouted from afar – as soon as they entered a carriage – and close at hand, unconcerned as to how many eardrums they shattered in the process.

And finally there were the beggars. Somehow they infiltrated the train and progressed through it, though it's hard to tell how, physically, they managed to do so. It was as if the Flying Mail – for that was the name of the train – had become a ghoulish means of transport for every conceivable and, even more, inconceivable form of human affliction. To say that legs and other major limbs were missing, that some had to crawl or be pulled along by another beggar, that bones and limbs and excrescences of flesh projected at impossible, hitherto undreamed-of angles, that sores and wounds covered and raged on whole bodies, that blindness was common and leprosy not unknown is hardly to begin to record the living horrors that paraded up and down the train, each with his or her own begging-bowl or -cup, each – at least those who could utter words – reciting noisily in Hindi the nature and cause of their condition.

The beggars would stop at each row of seats, and sometimes wait for what seemed an eternity, bowl or hand proffered. What was an eternity to this traveller was but a few seconds of life to those most horribly, cruelly, unfairly afflicted human beings. I know it sounds callous to say so, but if you start discriminating amongst beggars – do you give alms to those whose deformities you like the look of least, or most? – you can't cope with India, unless you are Mother Teresa of Calcutta or a millionaire. If you start doling out money to one, or a few, where do you draw the line? You will be harrowed endlessly, even purged; which may or may not be part of your reason for visiting the subcontinent. That you should be harrowed is the object of the exercise as far as the beggars are concerned, and that you should be made to feel guilty. Indeed, I do not believe it is entirely fantasy to wonder whether, on that journey to Amritsar, each and every mendicant was trying to outdo the previous one encountered in terms of the ghastliness, hopelessness of his or her condition.

How complacent, if not bitter, it is easy to become even

during the course of one train journey. I welcomed the approach of a blind man or woman because he or she was unable to see my face when the bowl was held out and I did not dispense largesse, providing myself with the (genuine) excuse that, as it was, I doubted whether my rupees and traveller's cheques would last for the length of my planned stay in the country. Most Indians seemed to manage to avoid giving alms without causing either offence or overt disappointment or seeming unduly, unfairly cornered. Is it simply cold-hearted or unimaginative to suggest that they'd grown immune to the whole act, the performance of the beggars; that they had to continue with their own lives?

I don't know where she came from but the girl – young woman – in a cotton sari of the most ravishing green was standing almost in front of me, a quite exceptional achievement in the circumstances. I say that her sari was green. It was a mixture of palette that Monet would have envied for his water-lily paintings. She was pointing the fingers of her left hand, encrusted with rings, into her open mouth. On a Western hand the rings would have looked theatrical and overdone. On her they were utterly appropriate, and somehow didn't contradict the nature of the gesture she was making, which was, presumably, a request for money with which to buy food. Her feet, I noticed, were unshod and elegantly shaped, with thick dull-silver bangles clinging to her ankles. The over-all effect was exotic and erotic.

She accompanied the gesture and the sentence she spoke with the word 'sir', not the more usual 'sahib'. As far as I could tell and had seen, I was the only Westerner on the train, certainly in this cattle-truck of a carriage. I was ripe to have my withers rung. Other beggars had, perhaps, seeing the colour of my skin, picked me out for special treatment but when they realised early on that I wasn't going to succumb they moved away. I was immediately mesmerised by the girl as if I were a moth unable to avoid its destiny on a burning light-bulb. No one around seemed even aware of the girl as she concentrated her efforts upon me. In one sense that was not particularly surprising as other

passengers throughout the journey had shown themselves
adept at ignoring the apparently endless procession of pet-
itioners. What was disturbing in her case was not that I
couldn't take my eyes away from her but the reason for this.
That in her case, alone of all the beggars, it wasn't because
of the ravages perpetrated upon her form but because of its
perfection.

For she was beautiful, her small features immaculately
shaped and placed. My eyes had found hers – they were
hardly difficult to seek out – and hers were staring into
mine. As I drowned in her cool dark pools she merely
besought me to give her a coin, a note. Merely? What is
merely to the impoverished?

It took me a little time to identify what was most bewilder-
ing about the girl, about the confrontation. She may have
been hungry and penniless but there was nothing physically wrong with her, at least not visibly so, not that I could
see. Had there been, presumably she would like the others
have made the most of it; unless pride dictated otherwise.
She was simply – simply! – a devastatingly attractive young
woman, a feast for the eyes of others, for my eyes. As I was
struggling in my exhausted mind to puzzle out the dicho-
tomy between her actions – of begging, being a beggar – and
her physical state of total grace she jerked her head down
towards my lap, placed her forehead across my knees. But
lightly, without leaning, without pressure.

Although none of the other passengers, crowded around
me, sitting and standing and on the racks above, reading,
talking, nodding off in the late-afternoon heat, gave the
impression of noticing what was happening – what had
happened – of being a witness, I was completely embarrassed. More than embarrassed: horrified. I wanted to
escape, be anywhere but where I was. If she were an ordinary beggar, I would not give her alms. Rather, I should have
given to the most hideous of her fellows. Was this my
punishment for not having done so? And if she were not an
ordinary beggar, what then? Who or what was she? I sat
stunned, quivering and sweating more freely even than

before in the impossible heat, as if in a hell – or did I mean a heaven, the obverse of the coin? – created by a Dickens or a Doré or a Peake. I wasn't particularly aware of having done so, but I must have closed my eyes – to try to escape from myself, from her, from the train – for when I opened them she had gone.

I still breathed. The train still moved. The world and its family still surrounded me, opposite, around, above. Sweat bathed my body, caused the few thin clothes I was wearing to cling to me as if they were a layer of skin, of flesh. Any intrusion upon my privacy, if such a condition could be thought attainable in such a public place, compounded my sense of horror at what had happened, the bud in the cancer. Not that it grew: it was total from the beginning, from when she first stood over me. And yet from that moment until she had gone could not have been longer than a minute, if that.

I tried to sleep, to put the heat and sweat, the lack of space which made it impossible for me to shift on my seat, the stifling aroma that clung to the air and clawed at people's clothes and bodies, the voices of vendors from the succession of pictures that crowded my mind – or the pulp that remained of it – as the train proceeded north-west and through the Punjab at its maddeningly leisurely pace. I tried to replace these images with one of her. More exactly, an image of her – she whom, in spite of myself, I desired to be consumed by – transcended the other pictures, was among them and superimposed upon them. Then she became a beggar, a beggar again from an angel, and not only because a supplicant. Was she drowning, like Ophelia, or falling out of the train in slow, slowest motion to a gory smeared ending? At that point in the airless, humid atmosphere I must have fallen asleep (for the first time or again?), or become unconscious, a more apt description in the context.

Then I woke up. Or, more precisely, was awakened. A fly, some sort of insect, was at my back, just above my waist. I felt it, whether in my state of drowsiness or by then awake I do not know. The fly was moving – in both directions, it seemed, upwards and downwards – and it felt heavy, closer to an animal than an insect. I moved my back as much as I could, wriggled a little to try to shed the encumbrance. It seemed to have gone, the fly, been dislodged. I lapsed into sleep again. I was between the two states, of consciousness and unconsciousness, and thought I would expire utterly if I didn't get out of the train soon, into some air. The journey was at least another two hours.

I felt it again. I must have been asleep. It had the weight, the force of a cat or a dog. Once more I tried to move, to shift, to break away, but as I leaned forward my head rubbed against the thighs of a man who had pushed in between me and the person sitting opposite. I leaned back. It had gone again, the touching, the pressure. Then a minute or two more of sleep – how can I know how long? – then the presence again, that pressure at my back, just above the waist but seeming to encompass a far greater area of my anatomy, as if it would mine and explode my body. Was there more than one insect, or animal, whatever it was? Suddenly I knew. It was a scorpion. I'd never felt nearer to wanting to be alive no more. This journey had gone on for ever. But a scorpion! I wanted to be snuffed out, not to linger. I knew that if I shouted or screamed no one would hear, or notice; that if I leaped to my feet I'd immediately be forced to sit down again as there was no space in which to stand.

Somehow, in the hopelessly confined space, I managed to turn my head. I was determined to trap the scorpion, whatever it was, to destroy it once and for all. This had been going on for hours, I felt (though I knew it was but minutes, if so long).

What I saw was an arm extended towards me, a human arm, and at the end of it a hand, fingers which were pushing me.

I turned away at once, reverted my gaze to the front, being too worn out even to consider how to cope with this latest horror. The fingers remained at my back, applying pressure but not varying it, only varying the areas of my back where they touched me. I mannaged to move away a bit, and the hand left my body. Indeed, whilst holding my head frontwards I could, looking down yet over my shoulder, observe the hand being withdrawn.

Again I dozed, faded into somnolence. Time passed, or it didn't. I had no idea as I was between being awake and asleep, half-awake, half-asleep. Then it was there again, the scorpion – no, the hand – and I managed to move my body in such a way that I could see behind me properly; it became possible. It was a small hand but not a child's; it was fully formed and moulded, a perfect hand, hung with rings. It was hers; I knew it was her hand, and the fingers were touching me, prodding my back, nudging it. At the same time the palm was open and held upwards, ready to receive alms, desirous to do so.

Again I wanted to scream, more than ever now; to tear myself out of the seat and wrench my mouth, the organs from my face, the head from my body; to wreck the train and ask everybody in it why no one was doing anything when they all, all must have seen; to leap out of the window and be gone, once and for all.

Instead, I twisted my left hand round behind my back and held hers, suddenly seized it, the hand that had been molesting me, and hurled it from me. There was a startled cry from behind the partition, the back of the row of seats on which I sat, and it may have been her cry but it wasn't a sound I would have associated with her from the few words I'd heard her speak, from what I'd seen of her. It wasn't a pretty sound. Besides, the noise of the train was such that I may have been misled, her crying out may have been distorted both by the other noises around and in my mind.

When I pushed, thrust the hand from me obviously I intended no more than that, that she should desist from disturbing me, interfering with my life. Clearly I didn't mean to detach it from its body, from her arm, the beautiful hand from the beautiful body. But that, extraordinary to relate in cold sobriety though it is, is what I am convinced happened. When I held the hand in mine I knew it was divorced from its natural body. You can tell the difference between the weight of a hand on its own compared with the weight of the same hand on its arm, an arm attached to a body. You just know; you don't have to have held a severed hand before.

I was terrified of what they would do to me, of what I had done to her, and then I was fully awake, my eyes gaping and staring with horror, with fear. I looked at the faces around. No passenger gave the impression of having seen what had happened, what I had inadvertently done.

I had to do something. I had to get out, get out, get out. I had to be gone before the hand was discovered and I was identified as its destroyer. I stood up, and somehow pushed my way to where she was standing, to where she had been standing behind me with only the back of the seat, the wooden partition between us. I saw her at once. She was unmistakable, her face, the green sari.

A baby was feeding at her right breast. With her left hand she was supporting and assisting the clinging infant. I forced myself to look down, to look at her right hand. Where it should have been. For blood, torn flesh and arteries. The arm was projecting from the sleeve of the sari, the part that served as the sleeve.

Her right hand, did I say? In its place was a withered stump, polished and shrunken like an old man's bald head. She had either been born without the hand or had lost it years ago, as a child, as a baby.

She saw me, saw me looking and angrily withdrew the arm up into the sari. Her eyes still begged, still besought me for money to buy sustenance, but she knew, as I did (a kind of horrific, ultimate irony), that she had no hand free to accept my tribute. Besides, the child was feeding off her.

I turned round, back to my seat. There was no question of my leaving the train. Someone was sitting where I had been. I stood for the remainder of the journey. She and her child got off long before we reached Amritsar.

A Mouthful of Gold

John Brunner

THE species Club Bore, made famous – or notorious – in so much Victorian and Edwardian fiction, is not, alas, extinct. My club, the Scriblerus, is the oldest literary club in London, and adheres to the ancient traditions; for instance, one eats at a long common table, and it's expected that one should take the next vacant place regardless of who will be seated alongside. This obviously gives great scope to the resident Bores, of whom I regret to say we have about half a dozen. They would probably suffice to drive most of the membership away, were it not for the club's truly miraculous wine-cellar. Its furniture is elderly; it needs redecorating; the only good chef we ever had retired three years ago; but, ah, the wine . . .!

Gilles Bertrand, of the French Embassy, whom I often invite there to dine with me, says he wishes desperately he were qualified to become a member, for the Scriblerus is the only place in London where the wine surpasses what he can get at home – 'home' being a moderately well-known château in the Loire valley with its own *appellation contrôlée*.

And I think I'm going to put him up for membership, because after what he did the other night to demolish Tulp, who is by a short head the least tolerable of our Bores, I warrant Gilles to be, if not a published author, at any rate a storyteller to match our best.

It went this way.

We were just commiserating over the underdone tapioca in the *potage velouté*, wondering whether the noticeable smell of burning from the kitchen had any relation to our next course of quails, and relishing the last few drops of a

Tête de Cuvée Le Montrachet, all at once, when Tulp sat down on my left. It was enough to make our expectations for the 1961 Saint-Emilion which we had ordered for the main course evaporate along with its bottle-stink.

As is the case in many clubs, there are certain subjects taboo at the table. How to keep writers from talking about money is a recurrent problem; however, it – along with sex, religion and politics – by custom is confined to the bar. Which has had to be enlarged twice in this century, but that's by the way; the old 'Ladies Room' where members were allowed to bring their wives or girl-friends was no loss, and half our committee consists of women writers now. A Good Thing.

I wish Tulp weren't among them, though.

Somehow around the time when her list of lovers exceeded the total of her published works, she went into business as a Professional Writer and *femme fatale*. She is enormously well read and well informed, but she can never overlook an opportunity to demonstrate the fact. This encounter proved no exception. While Gilles and I were giving silent thanks that the smoke from the kitchen was unrelated to our *cailles sur canapé* and that the wine had been blessed with a sound dry cork, Tulp regaled us with the long-winded account of how she had lately met again some tycoon in the business world who, when she was a naïve innocent, had attempted to dazzle her with a vision of caviare and champagne and luxury yachts. In front of her a glass of tonic-water lost its bubbles and a plateful of steak-and-kidney pie with boiled potatoes grew a glum brown skin of dried gravy while she described the affluence he had displayed and she had renounced 'for the sake of her art'. It was a little like hearing a first-hand report after the forty-days-in-the-wilderness bit, complete with a travelogue of the Kingdoms of the World.

Past a certain stage one is able to shut Tulp out like a half-heard radio in the next room. The gift I lack is to shut her *up*. Accordingly, once the quails were disposed of, Gilles and I looked sadly at one another and wordlessly decided to adjourn to the smoking-room for a Havana and an Armagnac. The Saint-Emilion had been superb, and no dessert should wipe it from the palate with a surplus of sugar.

'But you haven't heard the pay-off!' Tulp cried, stuffing her mouth with the by-now-revolting remains of her meal. A number of people elsewhere along the table looked coldly at her; for once, she took notice, and we were able to depart in peace.

Five minutes later she caught up with us and plumped – I choose my terms advisedly – into a leather armchair next to Gilles's.

As though there had been no hiatus, she exploded: 'But this time when I met him he was skint! Absolutely and completely! And serve him jolly well right!'

'Really?' said Gilles, in a tone I've learned to recognise as dangerous. He must be nearly sixty now, but he has the presence and energy of a much younger man, and his command of English makes me jealous. I shall never know, because I'm a little afraid to ask, why he has never been appointed to the rank of Ambassador, and will retire as First Secretary. Perhaps once in the distant past he did something at the wrong moment like what he did to Tulp at the right one.

'Skint?' he said reflectively, feigning to mishear the word. 'Ah, there are so few countries where a person can still be flayed for his crimes! But I met an old acquaintance once who was wearing only his bones, and the moment I set eyes on his skull I knew what name to put to it.'

'I said—' Tulp began. With flawless courtesy he went on talking as though she had not drawn breath.

'What's more, I connived at concealing his murder. And I never felt sorry about doing so. . . . Ah, thank you!' – to the waiter who delivered our coffee and brandy and the trolley with the cigars. Two or three people whom I'd introduced him to on earlier visits to the club fortunately came in at this juncture, and there was a distraction involving moving chairs and ordering drinks and smokes which I hoped would be enough to send Tulp in search of other prey. I was wrong. As soon as she had the chance, she began again doggedly.

'No – uh – monsieur. I didn't say "skinned", I said "skint". It's an English idiom. It means broke, bankrupt, without money.'

Tulp was cut out to be a pornographer. Her obsession with minutiae would have made her a grand success in the field.

'Ah, so!' Gilles said with a malicious twinkle, briefly becoming a parody Japanese. 'But the person I refer to, although deprived of his skin, retained a small fortune in solid gold which was no longer of use to him. However, I perceive I am holding the floor too long—'

'Go on! Go on!' chorused the new arrivals.

'Ah, but I am only a visitor, and—'

'*Go on!*' I said in exasperation, and handed him his brandy-balloon.

'At the risk of monopolising the conversation, then,' he said with a sigh, and leaned back in his high leather chair.

Late in 1944 I was in Italy, theoretically attached to the Goumiers regiment of Général Juin but – because I was fortunate in speaking a little Italian as well as tolerable English – doing a great deal of liaison work with the Canadians, whose breakthrough up the Liri valley had greatly contributed to the defeat of the Axis forces. Of course, one could no longer speak of the Axis by then. Mussolini was disgraced and his rump of a republic confined to an area around the northern lakes, while the Germans had not only the Allied invasion to cope with, but also Italian anti-Fascist partisans.

One might term it an interesting time, for as we marched north there was no way of telling whether what we would meet around the next corner would be the Germans, fighting inch by inch rather than retreat to the Alps as Rommel recommended, or the pro-Fascist Italians, or the anti-Fascist partisans who were on the Allied side, or the partisans who were on the Communist side and regarded us as invaders also. The partisans in general were the least trouble, but we were very cautious, and we made maximum use of aerial reconnaissance.

One pilot reported that in the next valley north he had seen a large number of people working in vineyards as though there was no war, and a few had waved white handkerchiefs on spotting his plane. Eager for any cheap advance over a ridge, my general detailed me to set off with a couple of jeeps and half a dozen men to check out this area.

The one available road was not even a cart-track; no cart could have negotiated the metre-size boulders we had to tip out of the way as we wound around the flank of the mountains. Obviously, since the outbreak of the war the vineyards on both sides had been tended by people on foot or at best on muleback. It was late in the year, as I said, and the grapes had long been picked, so we met no one until we crested the hill and began to descend.

On the far side we saw an old half-ruined château (as I would term it in French: a manor-house, you would say in English), with one wing either damaged by the war or tumbling down. This was on a small rise, and it was surrounded by a few fields where crops were planted, and many others where there were grape-vines trained on poles and wires. Though the harvest was in, twenty or so people, women, old men and boys, were at work, removing old shoots, training new ones, repairing rotten posts, and so forth. At the noise of our engines, and even more at the sight of our gunners weaving the machine-gun barrels back and forth while we scanned the landscape with binoculars, they all stopped what they were doing and began to wave white flags made of whatever came to hand. One girl even took off her petticoat – not that that was particularly white.

A tall woman separated herself from the rest and came down to stand at the roadside. She was as ill-clad as the others, in a torn blouse and a muddy skirt, but she called out to me in an educated accent instead of the local dialect.

'Are you Americans?' she asked.

I answered: 'No, I am French and these men are Canadians. But we are the forces of liberation.'

She looked me squarely in the eyes, and I shall never forget what an impression her face made. She was gaunt from war-time privation, but her cheekbones were like a sculptor's dream, and her eyes were dark and deep-set below a wide tanned brow. Her skin was heavily lined and hung loose below her chin, so she must have been at least fifty, but the merest glance revealed that she had once been a great beauty.

She said: 'My name is Signora Maler. It is not Italian. But it is not German. My husband Lodovico Maler is a prisoner of war in England. His family was proud of its Austro-Hungarian origins until the crazy Austrian Hitler betrayed us all.'

I knew that much of northern Italy had been under the Empire recently enough for foreign names to survive, so I simply nodded, promising to translate for the Canadian soldiers with me.

'We have done our best to protect a friend of yours against the Hun,' she said, and pointed up the hillside. The slanting sun – for this slope faced north-east, and even at noon the sunlight was moving away from it – showed me a young man with fair hair, in shabby peasant clothing, hobbling down towards us. He was tall, but he limped, and as he drew closer I saw he had a great scar, from a burn, all up the left side of his throat.

'He has been here months, and we have hidden him from the Germans, and it has not been easy. . . . But here you are, and praise be!'

By this time the young man was beside my jeep, and reaching out to shake my hand fervently. In a husky voice indicative of injury to his vocal cords, he forced out the statement that he was American, that he was called Henry J. Dyer, that he had been turret-gunner in a Flying Fortress, that it weren't no way such fun as shooting squirrels, that he came from Wisconsin and he was real glad to see us, yes sirree Bob!

Hearing him speak English, my companions hauled him into the jeep, and he grinned at us like a death's head. It was then that I saw he had four gold teeth in a peculiar pattern: one in the upper jaw, three in the lower with a natural tooth separating the first from the other two, all on the left side.

'Gee!' he said, and I believe that was the first time I heard anybody say that in real life, though I'd heard it in the many American gangster movies I'd watched. 'It sure is swell to be back with people who talk English instead of this dago stuff!'

And he added piously: 'But I guess that was what the Lord had in mind all along when he cast me among these idolaters.'

I said, rather foolishly: 'What?'

'Oh, they bow down to graven images and painted ones, too!' he said in that strained, somehow elderly voice. 'Just like I was warned against back home! *And* they drink liquor as though they weren't ashamed! The womenfolk, too! But' – his manner became suddenly virtuous – 'I never touched a drop, 'cept when it was forced down me 'cause I was too sick to stop 'em!'

At that moment my strict and proper duty was to turn right round and head back the way we'd come, to report that this valley at least was clear of Axis forces. But I was curious enough to interrogate Signora Maler, excusing the delay to myself on the grounds that she had mentioned protecting this American flier from the Germans.

It turned out that he had parachuted away from his burning plane on its way back from a raid and landed with a broken leg and a suppurating burn-mark on his neck – the scar of which remained – some three months earlier. Even though the area was full of Germans retreating from the Allied advance, they had tended him in the château – the big house – hiding him in the cellar at first, then when he was well enough to walk letting him out to join the grape-pickers; this for the survival of the Maler estate, rather than for his welfare, because their wine was all they had to finance next year's purchase of seed and pay their workers.

There had been one close call, when a German squad came this way and spotted him among the vines, but thanks to the scar on his throat it had been easy to make them believe he was deaf and dumb, particularly since he had only learned half a dozen words of Italian. 'He speaks', said Signora Maler contemptuously, 'like a three-year-old child!'

So that was a fine excuse why he was not serving with the Army. The Germans accordingly left him alone.

At about that point an enemy plane came roaring over – a Messerschmitt 410, as I recall – and we scrambled for cover. Luckily the slanting shadows created by the structure of the valley must have concealed the vehicles, for it flew on without noticing us. By the time the last echoes of its passage had died away, an elderly man with grizzled moustachios had arrived from the direction of the house carrying a bottle of wine and some mismatched glasses on a silver tray. Signora Maler insisted on pouring us all a drink, saying this was a wine her husband had reserved for the day when Mussolini was overthrown, if he should live so long.

It was superb! The mere couple of swigs the bottle afforded each of us was sufficient to let me realise that, like too many of my countrymen, I had always dismissed Italian wines as basically inferior, and was wrong. This was a *great* wine – not just fine, but *great*. And I was not prepared to spoil the mood it set, all by itself and on the instant, by demanding of Dyer why he accepted a glassful and then, sacrilegiously, poured it on the ground when he thought no one was looking. . . .

But the German plane had recalled me to duty, so we made our formal farewells and turned back, and the following day we were eight miles north of there by sunset, and the day after we were up among the Italian lakes and chasing out the last handful of Mussolini's supporters based around Lago di Garda.

I was compelled to suffer the company of Dyer until we ran across an American unit willing to take responsibility for him, and that was a relief, I may say, for he had attached himself to me like a stray lamb to a ewe in milk. I was regaled over and over with the tale of his experience among the heathens – which was precisely how he regarded the people who had taken him in, given him shelter, healed his wounds and kept him fed and safe. He was especially full of contempt for their farming practices. Apparently he was used to the wide fields of North America, and the whole mountainous landscape of the Alps and Apennines was for him a source of deep mistrust. Mixed in with his frequent utterances of praise to the Lord (for he was, as he spared no pains to remind us, raised in a Bible-reading, God-fearing home where the food was such as the angels enjoyed in Paradise – meaning buttermilk and cornbread, as near as I could make out) were sundry biased reflections on the work he had been given during his stay at the Castello Maler.

'Why, they set me to pluckin' grapes so shrivelled and wrinkled they was only fit to feed the hawgs!' he complained. 'I guess some of what they had was good fit eatin' grapes, but dawgoned little of 'em!'

It was the first time I had ever heard anyone actually say 'dawgoned'. A little later he became more emphatic, talking about the food – it seemed he disliked pasta regardless of what sauce was put on it – and advanced as far as 'dadblasted'. Somewhere around then I lost my patience with him and thus, I suppose, contributed indirectly to his death.

'Look!' I exclaimed. 'Those people risked their lives to save yours, don't you realise that? If the Germans had caught you, they might have treated you as a prisoner of war, but they would certainly have shot the people who sheltered you! Why, only a few weeks ago they massacred the entire population of a village called Sant' Anna di Stazzema, and that wasn't the first time they'd done such a thing! Instead of moaning about your saviours, you ought to be thinking what you can do in return!'

That, at least, got through to him. He thought about it a while, and eventually gave me a broad smile which displayed his gold teeth to maximum effect.

'Captain, you're dawgoned right!' he said. 'I guess them Eyeties did me more of a favour than I gave 'em credit for. And I figured out *egg-zackly* what I can do to pay 'em back. It'll have to wait until after the war, of course,' he added hastily.

I didn't imagine the people at Castello Maler were in any great hurry to see their American visitor again, so I just told him that was fine and changed the subject. And the following day we managed to palm him off on an American unit, as I said, and after that I more or less forgot about him. When I met him the next and final time, he was in no condition to say hello. . . .

It was more than ten years before I paid another visit to that part of Italy, around the lakes north of Verona. Then business took me from Milan to Vienna, and I had enough time to make a slow trip, so I rented a car, thinking I could relax and enjoy the scenery a little on the way. I hadn't reckoned with the weather. It poured! It pelted down! And somehow I missed a signpost and, although the road I was following was well metalled, it was narrow, and it wound like a drunken snake, so I had almost decided to turn back – all the way to Milan if necessary – when I rounded a bend and had to stop sharply. The rain had caused a minor landslip, not enough to block the road, but quite enough to make me get out with my coat pulled up over my head to walk a hundred metres and see if there were any more such hazards beyond the next hill.

I kicked at what I took to be a large lump of clay dislodged from the hillside, and it rolled over, and as the rain washed it free of mud it grinned at me.

I would have known those gold teeth anywhere. . . .

All of a sudden I knew where I was. The road had been so improved, I had not previously realised. I was no more than a kilometre from the Castello Maler, and since they had been so hospitable there to an American flier it seemed like a good idea to beg a night's lodging; it was getting dark by now.

And then I looked again at the skull, and belatedly began to wonder what the hell it was doing lying in the road. I must have been very tired, because what I did next seemed to me perfectly normal.

In the car I had a couple of plastic bags because I had bought the makings for a picnic lunch and not dared get out of the car to eat it, so dense was the downpour. I brought one of them and loaded the skull into it, and with it rocking back and forth on the seat beside me made my gingerly way to the Castello. It was where, and just as, I remembered it, except that the damaged wing had been repaired.

The sound of my engine brought an elderly woman rushing out with a cape over her, and I rolled down the window and announced myself, and asked whether Signora Maler was here. Letting go of the cape to cross herself, she told me no, *la signora* was dead. But, she added quickly, *il signore* was in residence. Was I a friend?

Assuming this must be a son who had inherited, I explained that I had been here once during the war, and the old woman exclaimed with excitement and insisted that I come indoors at once, leaving my baggage to be brought by one of the servants. She was positive that *il signore* would wish to welcome anyone who had fought against the Fascists.

So I went in, feeling like a bit of a fool, carrying the plastic bag because I was afraid to leave the skull where it was, but wishing I'd just kicked it down the hill! Why on earth, though, should Dyer have come back here to die?

In a handsome high-ceilinged room furnished with fine eighteenth- and nineteenth-century carved tables, chairs and cabinets, I was received not by a young man, but by an old one: lean, still handsome in a hawk-faced way, but white-haired and too weak, as he explained apologetically, to rise from his chair. He bade me be seated and sent the old woman for nuts and wine, which – as I awkwardly dumped the plastic bag beside my chair – I greatly looked forward to, remembering how good the wine had been which I sampled here on my visit during the war.

My host, as I had begun to suspect, was that Lodovico Maler who had been in a prison-camp in England at the time. Clearly his experiences had taken their toll; after we had exchanged initial politenesses, he explained that he had been injured before he was captured, and lain three days and nights without medical attention to a wound in his back which eventually affected his spinal cord. The British, he said, had done their best for him, but those three days had been crucial.

I learned, too, that his wife had died no more than a year before, at which I expressed my great sorrow, and then the old woman was back with our refreshments. Before I could prevent her, she had knocked the bag beside my chair with a careless foot, and the skull rolled just enough into view to be recognised. With a scream, and crossing herself again madly, she rushed from the room, while I sat wondering what in the world I had been thinking of when I decided to bring the thing indoors, rather than leaving it until I could find some tactful opportunity to broach the subject.

'I'm sorry,' I said foolishly. 'I found it on the road which runs alongside your vineyards to the south of here. I thought it unworthy that human remains should be disinterred by the weather, so I was going to ask whether you have a chapel or a vault or. . . .'

My improvisations sounded flimsy to my own ears, and the old man saw through them at once.

'Show me this skull,' he commanded, and I obeyed, leaving dribbles of dirty wetness on the fine tiled floor.

He stared at it for a long while; then, not looking at me, he said, 'There can be few men with gold teeth in such a pattern.'

'I only ever met one,' I said after a pause.

'And I also,' he said with a sigh. 'I will tell you the whole story. It is time for me to be judged. Put that thing away. It shall receive Christian interment whatever your verdict, I assure you.'

Complying, I felt my head full of dizzy visions. What could have happened? Obviously Dyer had kept his prom-

ise and returned after the war, but what had he done –
raped the wife, or the daughter if there was one? I covertly
glanced around in the hope of spotting family portraits to
afford a clue, but there were only a couple of landscapes in
oils.

While I was repacking the skull and wiping my hands on
my handkerchief, the old man creaked to his feet. I made to
help him but he brushed me aside. With terrible slowness
he made his way to a locked cabinet. He was wearing a full
suit, including a waistcoat and gold watch and chain. On
the chain hung some keys; he selected one, opened the
cabinet, and revealed an old and dusty bottle, its neck
sealed with ordinary sealing wax. Beside it stood a pair of
exquisite cut-crystal wine-glasses.

The old man reached for the bottle, then checked as he
saw how his hand shook.

'I must ask you to do me the service,' he said reluctantly.
'There is a knife, there is a corkscrew, there are glasses.
Open this bottle and pour for us, and I will tell you every-
thing.'

He returned to his chair with immense effort, slumped
into it and wiped his sweating forehead. Meantime,
puzzled, I took the bottle, which was of half-litre size, and
examined it. It bore no label and was of a dark-green glass,
so I could not guess at the contents.

Having struggled with the wax for a while, I broke most
of it away, and dutifully drew the cork. I had something of
the sensation a priest must have when performing a sacred
rite, for the old man was sitting gazing in rapture, hands
folded on his chest in an attitude almost of prayer.

And the moment the cork was out I realised I was indeed
in the presence of something at least magical. I have never
before or since known a wine to release so much bouquet at
the first instant! My mouth literally watered with excitement.

'Fill both glasses to the brim!' he commanded. 'Or – no,
mine a little less, for my hand's unsteady. And sit down
again.'

I did so, and with great formality he toasted me and we both sipped. Oh, the promise of the bouquet was more than fulfilled on the palate! I thought of sunrises, and fields of violets, and apricots dangling from the tree, and the shadow of angels' wings.

Abruptly, as though it were an alchemical potion, my mind went into high gear. I remembered what Signora Maler had said about her husband's family being of Austro-Hungarian origin, and I suddenly knew what this must be: a wine I had read about but never encountered, the only wine in all the world which is made without a wine-press, because the grapes are simply piled into an open cask with a hole at the bottom so the juice can drip out as they burst under their own weight.

With absolute conviction I said: 'Signor Maler, I am forever in your debt. For years I have hoped to taste the Tokaji Essencia, and at last I've done so.'

He gave me a queer sidelong look and said: 'I'm afraid you're wrong.'

I must have sat gaping like a stranded fish for long moments before I could take another sip of the delectable nectar. How could I be wrong? Everything about it matched the descriptions I'd read, and which I practically had by heart: 'a wine with little alcohol, sweeter than honey, with a wonderful bouquet and flavour, which will remain perfect, if not for ever, certainly longer than any of the fortified wines except Madeira'.

Eventually, smiling as at a private joke, Maler took pity on me. He said: 'Most of my vineyards are planted with Garganega, Trebbiano and Traminer stocks. But there is one in particular which faces south yet is exposed to winds from either side, and that one is planted with Furmint.'

Furmint! That very type of grape which in Hungary is used for the fine Tokaji! In awe, I said as I held my glass up to the light to relish the rich colour of its contents: 'So you make this yourself, here. I must congratulate you. It's like drinking pure gold.'

'We did,' Maler said curtly.

'What?'

'We did make it. This is the last bottle. Pour me some more. It is even better that I dreamed it would be.'

'But why do you no longer make it?' I demanded. 'Is it too expensive? Is it' – I gestured at the windows as I refilled our glasses – 'the weather, perhaps?'

'None of those. As well as the right grape, the right site, the right amount of sun and wind, there is another pre-requisite for the production of Tokaji Essencia.'

I snapped my fingers. 'The *pourriture noble!*' I exclaimed.

'Exactly. The noble rot. A mould which has been of more benefit to humanity than any of its kin save bread-yeast and *penicillium*. Related types to those found on the land my ancestors used to own by the Tissa river do occur in other countries north of the Alps, but to the best of my knowledge and belief no one but myself has ever established the authentic Hungarian strain so far south, and on the correct grape. I achieved that just before the war.'

As though by a premonition I heard again Dyer's queru-lous tones complaining about the grapes he had been obliged to pick, fit in his view only to feed pigs. . . .

'And when I returned from England in 1946', Maler con-tinued, 'I fully expected to carry on, and revive the family's fortunes. Luckily, in a way, I no longer had a son to provide for; both mine were killed on active service. But I have two daughters, and at that time they were not yet married, so I was greatly hoping for a bumper harvest and the chance to market my own version of the Essencia for the first time. Previously there had been so little, I gave it to our friends as name-day presents. Probably no more than forty or fifty people, all told, realised how completely I had succeeded. And that summer looked perfect for the noble rot.'

He sipped and savoured his wine, gazing into the past; he spoke as if to himself, seeming to have forgotten I was in the room.

'Then, one day, a light aircraft flew up our valley. I remember it clearly. It was an Auster, single-engined and with a high wing. We still had the reflexes ingrained by war, and those who did not run for shelter went anxiously outside to look at it. It "buzzed" us once or twice, as though reconnoitring, and we saw it had things like bombs under its wing. Also it was painted with the name of some company or other, which I couldn't quite read. But I recall how strange I felt seeing a private aircraft again, after so many wearing the livery of one or other air force. . . .

'And then, when the pilot had scouted his ground, it came down each of the slopes of our vineyards, one after the other, and from these things like bombs drifted down a sort of mist. Why I should have imagined that anybody wanted to attack us, I don't know, but I'm old enough to have served in the First World War, and we were drilled in anti-gas exercises in the Second, so the only thing I could think of – stupidly, I have to admit – was that someone, maybe a revanchist Fascist, was out to get us. I screamed for everybody, especially my wife and children, to take cover and breathe only through wet cloth. Thinking the war safely over, we had of course destroyed the few respirators we formerly possessed.

'But the plane kept well away from the house, and when we timidly emerged as its engine faded into the distance we found every single one of our grape-vines had been sprayed with a greenish liquid in tiny droplets. I must seem naïve, but please bear in mind that in the 1930s crop-spraying from the air was reserved to the world's wealthiest nations and, in spite of all, Italy was not one.

'Running to cover, I had seized a rifle, the first of my guns which came to hand. It was only a light sporting gun, but it felt comforting to have it in my grasp when I dared to venture out again. By now there was the noise of another engine, this time a car's labouring up the road to this *castello*. Then it was much as you remember it: a pot-holed track strewn with small boulders.

'But the driver made it, and halted his car before the house and got out, beaming with his mouth full of gold. I recognised him at once, for my wife had often told me about the American flier she and the estate staff had sheltered at the risk of being shot by the Germans, and who had been so rude and so ungrateful and so contemptuous.

'My wife spoke no English, and this man Dyer spoke no Italian; he was of the persuasion that, if you talk loud enough, foreigners will understand. Of course, in prison-camps in England I had learned at least a smattering of the language.

'He marched up to me and set his feet apart and his hands on his hips, and he shouted at me as though I were a backward child.

'He said: "The officer that took me away from here taught me a good lesson. Said I ought to do something to repay you folks for saving my life. I promised I would. And today I lived up to what I said. I been to Verona and I hired that there plane which just flew by, and I loaded it up with *the* latest copper-based fungicide from the good ol' U! S! of A! And, my frien's, y'aint never goin' to worry again about your grapes shrivellin' on the vine! No, suh! Not never, *nohow*!" '

Maler's hands were closing around his tiny fragile glass as though it were the stock of the sporting rifle he had been holding on that day. I think I already knew what he was about to tell me.

'So I shot him,' he said in a matter-of-fact voice. 'Just below the breast-bone, slanting up into the lower portion of the heart. He lived, I suppose, just long enough to realise that his gift was not appreciated, because a look of terrible surprise spread over his face before he fell down. But I reasoned that if his life had been saved by my people it was at my disposal.'

He drained his glass and held it out for more; the elixir seemed to be lending him fresh vigour.

'You did nothing of the kind,' I said when I had re-plenished both glasses; the bottle was still almost half-full. 'You had the gun in your hand with the safety-catch off, and your finger tightened at the shock of hearing that your life's work had been ruined by a well-meaning, but thick-headed, foreigner.'

He brightened instantly. 'You think so?' he demanded. 'I can almost hear my wife's voice again in what you say. She used to tell me that. But all I know – all I was able to tell my confessor – was that in that moment I *wanted* to kill him. Not just shoot him, but roast him slowly over a hot fire while someone explained to him in his own language what he had done.'

He shrugged lopsidedly as he took another drink, and concluded: 'Anyhow, we buried him at the far edge of the estate, little thinking the weather would expose his remains – though the soil here is shallow enough, the Lord knows! – and we also arranged for his hired car to be found abandoned at Gargnano. It was still a lawless and disorganised time, and not a few wealthy American visitors vanished without trace.'

I thought for a while, and finally I said: 'Even though he did me no harm, there was a time on the way back to my base when *I* wanted to kill him.'

'What's that you say?' Maler demanded.

'For his ingratitude,' I said firmly. 'And, if I hadn't told him what I thought of the way he was moaning about his treatment, he would still be alive today. Have I mentioned that my own family owns vineyards in France?'

From that moment on we were the firmest of friends. I've no idea what disposition was made of the skull in the end, but I remember I was a day late reaching Vienna and thereby lost the chance of an important business deal, but I didn't give a damn. I'm only sorry that Lodovico, as I shortly came to call him, was taken off by the next flu epidemic.

Yes?

For the past several minutes Gilles had adroitly been evading signs from Tulp to the effect that she wanted to interrupt. Now, finally, he was obliged to surrender to her insistence.

'It can't be true!' she blared in the frenzied tone of someone who has been desperately awaiting the chance to show off superior knowledge.

'What can't?' I demanded.

'The whole of this damned story!' she declared. 'I happen to know for a fact that in late 1944 the area around the Italian lakes, including Lago di Garda, was still under German occupation! Mussolini lasted until April 1945 with German protection! Allied troops can't have been anywhere near Verona or wherever you said you were!'

She sat back in bloated triumph. By now the circle of listeners was numerous and extensive, and all of us, including me, looked to Gilles with sympathy, for we had been completely caught up in his tale, and it seemed a shame for it to be thus demolished right at the end.

But he sat there unruffled, gazing down into his now empty brandy-glass.

'Well, naturally,' he said at length. 'Naturally I don't publicise the real location of that estate, because Lodovico left it to me in his will, and I'm pleased to say it has proved possible to repeat his work and the *pourriture noble* has been re-established on the proper Furmint grapes and any year now we may well have enough Essencia to put on the market. In the meantime' – and here he turned to me, smiling with a slight bow – 'there is a little which I reserve for particular friends, and perhaps I can let one or two of the people I know in London sample it before I go home. Speaking of going home, I think I ought to find a taxi.'

Tulp sat rock-still and turned – I swear it – purple, while the rest of us laughed, rose to our feet and dispersed. I saw Gilles to his cab, shook hands, said good-night – and *didn't* ask whether I might expect some Tokaji Essencia at Christmas.

But I'm certainly going to put him up for membership of the Scriblerus. Just in case.

Home Ownership

Murray Bail

THE insidious Habit of Thrift was proclaimed by the churches and the home-purchase pamphlets: '13,690 homes have been provided, another 605 are under construction.' That was the year ending 30 June 1934. All you needed was a deposit of £35. The houses were built on cedar stilts, Brisbane being such a humid city. It's the stilts and the galvanised iron which give Brisbane its temporary air as if the whole lot could be quickly dismantled or swept away.

The street began like all the rest littered with sharp-smelling sawdust and bent nails not yet rusty or trodden into the ground. The sewerage came later. All white, the row of wooden houses exuded a kind of transparent hope, definitely, like new glass. The ground all around was bare.

That was – what? Goodness, forty years back.

Like everything else, the street has changed.

Number 17 has the front porch converted into a sleep-out with louvred windows. Next door there, 'EMOH RUO', has the yellow carport leaning against the side.

Plenty of others have tacked on, if not another bedroom, something. There are metal blinds galore, house-names in inlaid mulga, portholes, lantern-lights near the doorbell, various weather-vanes and ornamental flyscreens.

After the war the street went through a slack phase; nothing much moved (changed). A nomadic period followed, rented accommodation, the appearance of solitary strangers.

And now – must be due to the exorbitant cost of new housing – young couples have returned, and there's been a spate of further extensions, 'improvements', shouting children at dusk, power-saws biting into the night. Only one house, Parker's there over the road, has remained as it was, motionless on its stilts, while the street and time passed it by. Parker couldn't be better-named! Since he moved in the week after he married he hasn't budged.

As a young man he rode a bike to work, the future before him. In those days he had yellow hair and an open blank expression. With their new house in the background Joyce would run out and wave, after first wiping her hands on her thighs: funny characteristic habit of hers. Then she'd remain for several minutes leaning over the gate, looking up and down. Other times, early in their marriage, she could be seen digging in the garden with a heart-shaped trowel.

Joyce cut back the wild grass and muck; carted away the builder's rubbish; and one weekend had Parker out there pouring concrete borders. Here she planted several cactus plants which threw geometric shadows at dusk. It was an attempt to impose order on the harsh elements, as if their lives would become ordered accordingly. This is common in Queensland. People dress very neatly.

Yet Joyce certainly wasn't the person one normally associates with cactus. The house wore brightly coloured curtains. On certain afternoons the windows reflected the trees and passing clouds just like her sunglasses, while the door in between kept opening and closing. With the step painted veranda-red, the house had a look . . . very conscious of itself. Joyce had this other funny habit, noticeable even from a distance. After saying something, usually to a man, she'd roll her lips back as if she'd committed an error or was applying lipstick. A nervous habit. She was short, firm-breasted. She had large eyes. Oh, she was something! Joyce always liked to laugh. At the same time she was serious. She could be hard on Parker some days – waiting for him the minute he stepped in. He, the pedalling Methodist, without a tie but with the top button done up. He had a simple wooden expression. It implied stubbornness. Where did they meet? A ludicrous doomed pair. Couldn't everyone see that?

Brisbane hummed with a kind of humid emptiness. It drove people with a perfectly sound mind to drink. The slow-moving days were punctuated at metronomic intervals by door-to-door salesmen. The ring on Parker's bell was the signal, though often as not the house would be wide open.

The house breathed through the door.

'I say, anybody home? You-who!'

And then came the murmur of Joyce's time-consuming idle questions; at intervals her sudden high laugh.

There was nothing else to do in Brisbane.

Raising one trousered leg on the step, arms and jaws all working in unison, the reps altered the geometry of the foreground. Most of them were hard-working with mortgages of their own, and it was noticeable how after a while most of them took to avoiding Joyce's door. She never bought a thing.

There was one particular regular who peddled American pens and propelling pencils, all colours, in rows like picket fences. His narrow sample-case was lined with them.

This man had a hungry tanned neck, wiry wrists – loose gold watch – and wore brown suit-trousers. He had lizard eyes. The eyes of a lizard: sliding off while selling half-heartedly, more interested in her over the road bending in the garden. He let out a loud conspiratorial laugh without foundation, and Joyce glanced up. You could see what he was up to. Few weeks later, sure enough, he was in there, leg up on the step, his suitcase of pens not even opened. Shielding her eyes, Joyce had a way of squinting: her hand apexed over eyes duplicated the shape of the peaked roof sheltering the windows.

Every second Thursday he called. Regular as clockwork.

He liked to say, 'I'll toddle off now to Mrs Cactus,' and wink. He called her Mrs Cactus.

A familiarity did grow between them. He was a traveller of sorts. He had endless stories. She took to sitting casually, ostentatiously, on his suitcase, exposing the red step of the open door. Clasping one knee as they did in those days, she leaned back and laughed. Some afternoons she wore pale-blue shorts.

He told lies about himself, lies a woman recognises and yet laughs. They were for her.

She liked to laugh.

With Parker she didn't have much of a chance.

Some Friday afternoons he began appearing without calling on other houses; and every other Thursday Joyce would be there wandering casually around near the gate, expectant. Coatless in summer, leaning against the house, that shirt of his merged into the white weatherboard. All that was visible then was his tanned head. She'd come out with what looked like lime cordial or tea. For several hours he'd stay. Parker usually worked overtime on Fridays. And the house with its picket fence maintained a dental smile, no sign of decay.

There was nothing much wrong with what they were doing – sitting on the steps – yet the women who'd liked Joyce before seemed to think so. They shied away and pulled faces at the slightest pretext. Perhaps they were right; because Joyce took no notice. And he no longer bothered even bringing his sample-case. It turned out later he had lost his job.

Strange how 1939, fateful year for the world, was on a smaller scale a fateful year for the Parkers.

Underneath these Brisbane houses people store their tools and ladders, fruit for preserves, bits of timber and junk in shadows bordered by the stilts. To camouflage the mess, white lattice covers the front and sides, perforating the shadows. It's dark and cool underneath.

At about four one afternoon he emerged from there, and returned casually to his place on the steps. A little later Joyce followed and went inside. He turned to say something, but she had shut the door. The exact day is easily remembered. Hitler's armies had poured into Poland, a Friday.

Emptied, made plain, devastated by the war, the street like

many others in Brisbane took an age to recover. The street seemed wider, but of course it wasn't.

Parker's house was still there; it seemed to have tilted slightly. This was another optical illusion. The under-growth and the turbulent dead sticks which had been allowed to go wild after Joyce's death formed shoulders across the foreground, obliterating the stilts and lattice, one shoulder higher than the other. It came as a shock: it had overwhelmed Joyce's cactus, darkened the face of the house. Nothing had been done to lift the fallen front gutter, and the first time it rained, in 1945, it shed three separate streams of water.

Joyce had been pregnant, as everybody knew. Poor girl. She was found in the bathroom, sometime early 1940. Cir-cumstances remain vague. But complications occurred more in those days. Parker, of course, had always wanted children, actually talking about five. He was a fool.

Joyce was twenty-eight.

The front door had opened and closed a few times, then it remained shut. There was no light. Parker preferred the back, the kitchen, at night.

His punctuality became a joke. He hardly spoke.

With its hooded eyes, jowls, resting on its dry shoulders, the house stubbornly gazed. It was always there. Lily-white in Joyce's day, its complexion beginning to deteriorate, the former pinkish glow at the end of the day assuming a kind of ashen grey. Unattended, the paint-skin began falling away, in Parker's case revealing raw patches; it can be the problem with weatherboards. The red step, that character-istic spot alive in the centre, chafed and faded. No longer was it the focal point. Nothing was. At five o'clock a slate-coloured shadow grew below the windows and spread, and over the years darkened considerably.

Parker stopped going to church. He over-reacted, it was said.

Dandruff spotted his shoulders, He had filled out con-siderably: wide dark shoulders. His hair thinned and turned a kind of rust-brown. Short, back and sides. When he came out and stumbled along unshaven, unkempt, it was with his kitbag to buy groceries. Some of his front teeth had gone.

It was said he had gone soft in the head.

The eyebrows darkened as weeds grew and withered in the gutters, drooping over the twin miniature roofs shading the front windows. These jutted either with stubbornness or a kind of blindness. The windows beneath retreated into the shadows, never cleaned. The frown which developed was caused there by the line of wooden slats above the windows, and the angle of the fallen main gutter. Slowly the picket fence lost its smile. It had always been inane, irritating, anyway. Palings turned grey and here and there loosened by humidity and time angled and fell away: dark spaces, gaping holes, were displayed. Sometime in the fifties Parker had to wear glasses. Parker had an unusually lined and weathered face for his age. As time passes, it takes an effort to maintain appearances.

Grey weeds appeared, most noticeably out of the chimney.

The nose seemed to lengthen. They do with age. It grew dark, a blue-grey, and in the morning dripped for several hours.

Parker didn't seem to care.

Parker seemed merely to continue, passing through the house and time. It was a life.

Perhaps inevitably, the plumbing gave trouble. Quite an operation digging around the foundations; quite a stench, too, of soaked earth and ruptured pipes. It had to be done.

Parker had hardly missed a day's work in his life.

There was the Vietnam war in the late sixties.

Certainly, the roof showed signs of age. Apart from the gutters which suddenly overflowed without control or warning, a few of the corrugated sheets and the ridge-cap lifted in the slightest breeze, and rust, first freckles, then beer-coloured streaks became dark scabs: another darkening process. The roof was egg-shell thin. And of course early on parts of the lattice had gaping holes, evidently rotten below the shoulders, like one of Parker's Swedish singlets.

He withdrew farther into the house, so it seemed, retreating behind shadows and that shemozzle in the foreground, and small boys sometimes crept up and rang the bell or threw stones on the roof. It naturally attracted attention, increasingly so, as the other houses became renovated. A sign in green biro, 'NO HAWKERS', appeared on the gate, although door-to-door salesmen, if you don't count the Mormons, haven't appeared in years and, even if they had, it's doubtful they would have called.

The various horizontal lines had filled with dirt and moved apart, no longer parallel but wandered and concentrated around the shut mouth and the dull windows and, what with additional cracks and unexpected shadows, formed a network of wrinkles, a stubborn complexity. A kind of weariness grew as the house brooded, which was not obvious before. More and more it drooped. After all, he couldn't care less. It was futility. It happened gradually until one day it became clear and stayed that way. The steps, now grey, blurred into a jutting chin.

So he passed the years, inside.

Suddenly registering one morning, like the rare appearance of Parker along the footpath, was the bulge on the right-hand side, quite a rupture, a weakness there. And it's still there today. That can be a problem with the old weatherboards.

Parker put his bike away. Under the house. Not long after, he retired. That was only a few years ago.

He kept his thoughts to himself.

Dark birds as small as flies buzzed around the mouth. A blocked chimney became a recurring minor trouble and, beginning around March, the bathroom became incontinent, quite unreliable. Other gutters slipped at the side.

It settled on its shoulders, its eyes almost closed.

A vibration, a tic, developed and accelerated even in the still conditions of Brisbane. It was that loose downpipe, the skinny elbow on the right.

And now this, or at last: unknown to Parker, or to anyone else in the street, white ants had been at the insides, destroying and multiplying, attacking beneath the surfaces. Evidently it had been going on for some time. The collapse when it came was sudden and complete. It has come as a shock. For a long time, almost since the war, it seemed no one had really been living there, and now there's only a house.

Chemistry

Graham Swift

THE pond in our park was circular, exposed, perhaps fifty yards across. When the wind blew, little waves travelled across it and slapped the paved edges, like a miniature sea. We would go there, Mother, Grandfather and I, to sail the motor-launch Grandfather and I made out of plywood, balsawood and dope-smothered paper. We would go even in the winter – especially in the winter, because then we would have the pond to ourselves – when the leaves on the two willows turned yellow and dropped and the water froze your hands. Mother would sit on a wooden bench set back from the perimeter; I would prepare the boat for launching. Grandfather, in his black coat and grey scarf, would walk to the far side to receive it. For some reason it was always Grandfather, never I, who went to the far side. When he reached his station I would hear his 'Ready!' across the water. A puff of vapour would rise from his lips like the smoke from a muffled pistol. And I would release the launch. It worked by a battery. Its progress was laboured but its course steady. I would watch it head out to the middle while Mother watched behind me. As it moved it seemed that it followed an actual existing line between Grandfather, myself and Mother, as if Grandfather were pulling us towards him on some invisible cord, and that he had to do this to prove we were not beyond his reach. When the boat drew near him he would crouch on his haunches. His hands – which I knew were knotted, veiny and had on them little mottles that were the result of an accident in one of his chemical experiments – would reach out, grasp it and set it on its return.

The voyages were trouble-free. Grandfather improvised a wire grapnel on the end of a length of fishing-line in case of shipwrecks or engine failure, but it was never used. Then one day – it must have been soon after Mother met Ralph – we watched the boat, on its first trip across the pond to Grandfather, suddenly become deeper and deeper in the water. The motor cut. The launch wallowed, sank. Grandfather made several throws with his grapnel and pulled out clumps of green slime. I remember what he said to me, on this, the first loss in my life that I had witnessed. He said, very gravely, 'You must accept it. You can't get it back. It's the only way,' as if he were repeating something to himself. And I remember Mother's face as she got up from the bench to leave. It was very still and very white, as if she had seen something appalling.

It was some months after that that Ralph, who was now a regular guest at weekends, shouted over the table to Grandfather: 'Why don't you leave her alone?'

I remember it because that same Saturday Grandfather recalled the wreck of my boat, and Ralph said to me, as if pouncing on something: 'How about me buying you a new one? How would you like that?' And I said, just to see his face go crestfallen and blank, 'No!', several times, fiercely. Then as we ate supper Ralph suddenly barked, as Grandfather was talking to Mother: 'Why don't you leave her alone?'

Grandfather looked at him. 'Leave her alone? What do you know about being left alone?' Then he glanced from Ralph to Mother. And Ralph didn't answer, but his face went tight and his hands clenched on his knife and fork.

And all this was because Grandfather had said to Mother: 'You don't make curry any more , the way you did for Alec, the way Vera taught you.'

It was Grandfather's house we lived in – with Ralph as ever-more-permanent lodger. Grandfather and Grandmother had lived in it almost since the day of their marriage.

My grandfather had worked for a firm which manufactured gold- and silver-plated articles. My grandmother died suddenly when I was only four; and all I know is that I must have had her looks. My mother said so and so did my father; and Grandfather, without saying anything, would often gaze curiously into my face.

At this time Mother, Father and I lived in a new house some distance from Grandfather's. Grandfather took his wife's death very badly. He needed the company of his daughter and my father; but he refused to leave the house in which my grandmother had lived, and my parents refused to leave theirs. There was bitterness all round, which I scarcely appreciated. Grandfather remained alone in his house, which he ceased to maintain, spending more and more time in his garden shed which he had fitted out for his hobbies of model-making and amateur chemistry.

The situation was resolved in a dreadful way: by my own father's death.

He was required now and then to fly to Dublin or Cork in the light aeroplane belonging to the company he worked for, which imported Irish goods. One day, in unexceptional weather conditions, the aircraft disappeared without trace into the Irish Sea. In a state which resembled a kind of trance – as if some outside force were all the time directing her – my mother sold up our house, put away the money for our joint future, and moved in with Grandfather.

My father's death was a far less remote event than my grandmother's, but no more explicable. I was only seven. Mother said, amidst her adult grief: 'He has gone to where Grandma's gone.' I wondered how Grandmother could be at the bottom of the Irish Sea, and at the same time what Father was doing there. I wanted to know when he would return. Perhaps I knew, even as I asked this, that he never would, that my childish assumptions were only a way of allaying my own grief. But, if I really believed Father was gone for ever, I was wrong.

Perhaps, too, I was endowed with my father's looks no less than my grandmother's. Because when my mother looked at me she would often break into uncontrollable tears and she would clasp me for long periods without letting go, as if afraid I might turn to air.

I don't know if Grandfather took a secret vengeful delight in my father's death, or if he was capable of it. But fate had made him and his daughter quits and reconciled them in mutual grief. Their situations were equivalent: she was a widow and he a widower. And just as my mother could see in me a vestige of my father, so Grandfather could see in the two of us a vestige of my grandmother.

For about a year we lived quietly, calmly, even content-edly within the scope of this sad symmetry. We scarcely made any contact with the outside world. Grandfather still worked, though his retirement age had passed, and would not let Mother work. He kept Mother and me as he might have kept his own wife and son. Even when he did retire we lived quite comfortably on his pension, some savings and a widow's pension my mother got. Grandfather's health showed signs of weakening – he became rheumatic and sometimes short of breath – but he would still go out to the shed in the garden to conduct his chemical experiments, over which he hummed and chuckled gratefully to himself.

We forgot we were three generations. Grandfather bought Mother bracelets and earrings. Mother called me her 'little man'. We lived for each other – and for those two unfaded memories – and for a whole year, a whole har-monious year, we were really quite happy. Until that day in the park when my boat, setting out across the pond towards Grandfather, sank.

Sometimes when Grandfather provoked Ralph I thought Ralph would be quite capable of jumping to his feet, reaching across the table, seizing Grandfather by the throat and choking him. He was a big man, who ate heartily, and I was often afraid he might hit me. But Mother somehow kept him in check. Since Ralph's appearance she had grown neglectful of Grandfather. For example – as Grandfather had pointed out that evening – she would cook the things that Ralph liked (rich thick stews, but not curry) and forget to produce the meals that Grandfather was fond of. But, no matter how neglectful and even hurtful she might be to Grandfather herself, she wouldn't have forgiven someone else's hurting him. It would have been the end of her and Ralph. And no matter how much she might hurt Grandfather – to show her allegiance to Ralph – the truth was she really did want to stick by him. She still needed – she couldn't break free of it – that delicate equilibrium that she, he and I had constructed over the months.

I suppose the question was how far Ralph could tolerate not letting go with Grandfather so as to keep Mother, or how far Mother was prepared to turn against Grandfather so as not to lose Ralph. I remember keeping a sort of equation in my head: If Ralph hurts Grandfather, it means I'm right – he doesn't really care about Mother at all; but, if Mother is cruel to Grandfather (though she would only be cruel to him because she couldn't foresake him), it means she really loves Ralph.

But Ralph only went pale and rigid and stared at Grandfather without moving.

Grandfather picked at his stew. We had already finished ours. He deliberately ate slowly to provoke Ralph.

Then Ralph turned to Mother and said: 'For Christ's sake, we're not waiting all night for him to finish!' Mother blinked and looked frightened. 'Get the pudding!'

You see, he liked his food.

Mother rose slowly and gathered our plates. She looked at me and said, 'Come and help me.'

In the kitchen she put down the plates and leaned for several seconds, her back towards me, against the draining-board. Then she turned. 'What am I going to do?' She gripped my shoulders. I remembered these were just the words she'd used once before, very soon after Father's death, and then, too, her face had had the same quivery look of being about to spill over. She pulled me towards her. I had a feeling of being back in that old impregnable domain which Ralph had not yet penetrated. Through the window, half-visible in the twilight, the evergreen shrubs which filled our garden were defying the onset of autumn. Only the cherry-laurel bushes were partly denuded – for some reason Grandfather had been picking their leaves. I didn't know what to do or say – I should have said something – but inside I was starting to form a plan.

Mother took her hands from me and straightened up. Her face was composed again. She took the apple-crumble from the oven. Burned sugar and apple juice seethed for a moment on the edge of the dish. She handed me the bowl of custard. We strode, resolutely, back to the table. I thought: Now we are going to face Ralph; now we are going to show our solidarity. Then she put down the crumble, began spooning out helpings and said to Grandfather, who was still tackling his stew: 'You're ruining our meal. Do you want to take yours out to your shed?!'

Grandfather's shed was a more substantial structure than 'shed' suggests. Built of brick in one corner of the high walls that girt the garden, it was large enough to accommodate a stove, a sink, an old armchair, as well as Grandfather's work-benches and apparatus, and to serve – as it was serving Grandfather more and more – as a miniature home.

I was always wary of entering it. It seemed to me, even before Ralph, even when Grandfather and I constructed the model launch, that it was somewhere where Grandfather went to be alone, undisturbed, to commune perhaps, in some obscure way, with my dead grandmother. But that evening I did not hesitate. I walked along the path by the ivy-clad garden wall. It seemed that his invitation, his loneliness were written in a form only I could read on the dark-green door. And when I opened it he said: 'I thought you would come.'

I don't think Grandfather practised chemistry for any particular reason. He studied it from curiosity and for solace, as some people study the structure of cells under a microscope or watch the changing formation of clouds. In those weeks after Mother drove him out I learned from Grandfather the fundamentals of chemistry.

I felt safe in his shed. The house where Ralph now lorded it, tucking into bigger and bigger meals, was a menacing place. The shed was another, a sealed-off world. It had a salty, mineral, unhuman smell. Grandfather's flasks, tubes and retort-stands would be spread over his work-bench. His chemicals were acquired through connections in the metal-plating trade. The stove would be lit in the corner. Beside it would be his meal-tray – for, to shame Mother, Grandfather had taken to eating his meals regularly in the shed. A single electric light-bulb hung from a beam in the roof. A gas-cylinder fed his bunsen. On one wall was a glass-fronted cupboard in which he grew alum and copper sulphate crystals.

I would watch Grandfather's experiments. I would ask him to explain what he was doing and to name the contents of his various bottles.

And Grandfather wasn't the same person in his shed as he was in the house – sour and cantankerous. He was a weary, ailing man who winced now and then because of his rheumatism and spoke with quiet self-absorption.

'What are you making, Grandpa?'

'Not making – changing. Chemistry is the science of change. You don't make things in chemistry – you change them. Anything can change.'

He demonstrated the point by dissolving marble chips in nitric acid. But he went on: 'Anything can change. Even gold can change.'

He poured a little of the nitric acid into a beaker, then took another jar of colourless liquid and added some of its contents to the nitric acid. He stirred the mixture with a glass rod and heated it gently. Some brown fumes came off.

'Hydrochloric acid and nitric acid. Neither would work by itself, but the mixture will.'

Lying on the bench was a pocket watch with a gold chain.

I knew it had been given to Grandfather long ago by my grandmother. He unclipped the chain from the watch, then, leaning forward against the bench, he held it between two fingers over the beaker. The chain swung. He eyed me as if he were waiting for me to give some sign. Then he drew the chain away from the beaker.

'You'll have to take my word for it, eh?'

He picked up the watch and reattached it to the chain.

'My old job – gold-plating. We used to take real gold and change it. Then we'd take something that wasn't gold at all and cover it with this changed gold so it looked as if it was all gold – but it wasn't.'

He smiled bitterly.

'What are we going to do?'

'Grandpa?'

'People change, too, don't they?'

He came close to me. I was barely ten. I looked at him without speaking.

'Don't they?'

He stared fixedly into my eyes, the way I remembered him doing after Grandmother's death.

'They change. But the elements don't change. Do you know what an element is? Gold's an element. We turned it from one form into another, but we didn't make any gold – or lose any.'

Then I had a strange sensation. It seemed to me that Grandfather's face before me was only a cross-section from some infinite stick of rock, from which, at the right point, Mother's face and mine might also be cut. I thought: Every face is like this. I had a sudden giddying feeling that there is no end to anything. I wanted to be told simple precise facts.

'What's that, Grandpa?'

'Hydrochloric acid.'

'And that?'

'Green vitriol.'

'And that?' I pointed to another, unlabelled jar of clear liquid, which stood at the end of the bench, attached to a complex piece of apparatus.

'Laurel water. Prussic acid.' He smiled. 'Not for drinking.'

It was cold that night. All that autumn was exceptionally cold. I thought: Grandfather will die this winter. Shut in that cold outhouse, he will die. That is what they want. And yet how could I think this when something else was equally plain to me? Death did not exist. Grandfather knew that Grandmother wasn't dead, and Mother knew – though she was trying to forget – that Father wasn't dead. We all knew there was this apparent change, this apparent ending. . . .

Hadn't that been the basis, for a whole year, of our devotion to each other?

And then it occurred to me why Mother needed Ralph. He was big and fleshy – quite different from the slender, spare build of our family. He loved physical comfort and filling his belly. He had nothing of the ghost about him.

The evenings were chill and full of the rustlings of leaves. When I returned to the house from taking out Grandfather's meal-tray (this had become my duty) I would observe Mother and Ralph in the living-room through the open kitchen hatchway. They would drink a lot from the bottles of whisky and vodka which Ralph brought in and which at first Mother made a show of disapproving. The drink made Mother go soft and heavy and blurred, and it made Ralph gain in authority. They would slump together on the sofa. One night I watched Ralph pull Mother towards him and hold her in his arms, his big frame almost enveloping her, and Mother saw me, over Ralph's shoulder, watching from the hatchway, and she looked trapped and helpless.

And that was the night that I got my chance – when I went to collect Grandfather's tray. When I entered the shed he was asleep in his chair, his plates, barely touched, on the tray at his feet. In his slumber – his hair dishevelled, mouth open – he looked like some torpid captive animal that has lost even the will to eat. I had taken an empty spice-jar from the kitchen. I took the glass bottle labelled HNO_3 and poured some of its contents, carefully, into the spice-jar. Then I picked up Grandfather's tray, placed the spice-jar beside the plates and carried the tray to the house.

I thought I would throw the acid in Ralph's face at breakfast. I didn't want to kill him. It would have been pointless to kill him, since death is a deceptive business. I wanted to spoil his face so Mother would no longer want him. I took the spice-jar to my room and hid it in my bedside cupboard. In the morning I would smuggle it down in my trouser pocket. I would wait. Under the table I would remove the stopper. As Ralph gobbled down his eggs and fried bread. . . .

I thought I would not be able to sleep. From my bedroom window I could see the dark square of the garden and the little patch of light cast from the window of Grandfather's shed. Often I could not sleep until I had seen that patch of light disappear and I knew that Grandfather had shuffled back to the house and slipped in, like a stray cat, at the back door.

But I must have slept that night, for I do not remember seeing Grandfather's light go out or hearing his steps on the garden path.

That night Father came to my bedroom. I knew it was him. His hair and clothes were wet, his lips were caked with salt; seaweed hung from his shoulders. He came and stood by my bed. Where he trod, pools of water formed on the carpet and slowly oozed outwards. For a long time he looked at me. Then he said: 'It was her. She made a hole in the bottom of the boat, not big enough to notice, so it would sink – so you and Grandfather would watch it sink. The boat sank – like my plane.' He gestured to his dripping clothes and encrusted lips. 'Don't you believe me?' He held out a hand to me, but I was afraid to take it. 'Don't you believe me? Don't you believe me?' And as he repeated this he walked slowly backwards towards the door, as if something were pulling him, the pools of water at his feet drying instantly. And it was only when he had disappeared that I managed to speak and said: 'Yes. I believe you. I'll prove it.'

And then it was almost light, and rain was dashing against the window as if the house were plunging under water, and a strange small voice was calling from the front of the house – but it wasn't Father's voice. I got up, walked out on to the landing and peered through the landing window. The voice was a voice on the radio inside an ambulance which was parked with its doors open by the pavement. The heavy rain and the tossing branches of a rowan-tree obscured my view, but I saw the two men in uniform carrying out a stretcher with a blanket draped over it. Ralph was with them. He was wearing his dressing-gown and pyjamas, and slippers over bare feet, and he carried an umbrella. He fussed around the ambulancemen like an overseer directing the loading of some vital piece of cargo. He called something to Mother, who must have been standing below, out of sight at the front door. I ran back across the landing. I wanted to get the acid. But then Mother came up the stairs. She was wearing her dressing-gown. She caught me in her arms. I smelt whisky. She said: 'Darling. Please, I'll explain. Darling, darling.'

But she never did explain. All her life since then, I think, she has been trying to explain, or to avoid explaining. She only said: 'Grandpa was old and ill; he wouldn't have lived much longer anyway.' And there was the official verdict: suicide by swallowing prussic acid. But all the other things that should have been explained – or confessed – she never did explain.

And she wore, beneath everything, this look of relief, as if she had recovered from an illness. Only a week after Grandfather's funeral she went into Grandfather's bedroom and flung wide the windows. It was a brilliant, crisp late-November day and the leaves on the rowan-tree were all gold. And she said: 'There, isn't that lovely?'

The day of Grandfather's funeral had been such a day – hard, dazzling, spangled with early frost and gold leaves. We stood at the ceremony, Mother, Ralph and I, like a mock version of the trio – Grandfather, Mother and I – who had once stood at my father's memorial service. Mother did not cry. She had not cried at all, even in the days before the funeral when the policemen and the officials from the coroner's court came, writing down their statements, apologising for their intrusion and asking their questions.

They did not address their questions to me. Mother said: 'He's only ten. What can he know?' Though there were a thousand things I wanted to tell them – about how Mother banished Grandfather, about how suicide can be murder and how things don't end – which made me feel that I was somehow under suspicion. I took the jar of acid from my bedroom, went to the park and threw it in the pond.

And then after the funeral, after the policemen and officials had gone, Mother and Ralph began to clear out the house and to remove the things from the shed. They tidied the overgrown parts of the garden and clipped back the trees. Ralph wore an old sweater which was far too small for him and I recognised it as one of Father's. And Mother said: 'We're going to move to a new house soon – Ralph's buying it.'

I had nowhere to go. I went to the park and stood by the pond. Dead willow leaves floated on it. Beneath its surface was a bottle of acid and the wreck of my launch. But though things change they aren't destroyed. It was there, by the pond, when dusk was gathering and it was almost time for the park gates to be locked, as I looked to the centre where my launch sank, then up again to the far side, that I saw him. He was standing in his black overcoat and his grey scarf. The air was very cold and little waves were running across the water. He was smiling, and I knew: the launch was still travelling over to him, unstoppable, unsinkable, along that invisible line. And his hands, his acid-marked hands, would reach out to receive it.

Egnaro

M. John Harrison

EGNARO is a secret known to everyone but yourself.

It is a distant country, or some city to which you have never been; it is an unknown language. At the same time it is like being cuckolded, or plotted against. It is a part of the universe of events which will never wholly reveal itself to you: a conspiracy the barest outline of which, once visible, will gall you for ever.

It is in conversations not your own (so I learned from Lucas) that you first hear of Egnaro, and in situations peripheral to your real life. Egnaro reveals itself in minutiae, in that great and very real part of our lives when we are doing nothing important. You wait outside the library in the rain; an advert for a new kind of vacuum pump, photographed against a background of cycads and conifers, catches your eye. 'Branch offices everywhere!' Old men sit on the park benches, and as you pass make casual reference to some forgotten campaign in the marshes of a steamy country. You are always in transit when you hear of Egnaro, in transit or in limbo. A book falls open, and you read with a sudden inexpressible *frisson* of nostalgia: 'Will I ever return there?' (Outside, rain again, falling into someone else's garden; a wet black branch touches the window in the wind.) A woman at a dinner party murmurs: 'Egnaro, where the long sunlit esplanades lift from a wine-dark sea. . . .'

It is this overheard fragmentary quality which is so destructive. By the time you have turned your head the woman is speaking of tomatoes and hot-house flowers; someone has switched off the news broadcast with its hints

of a foreign war; the accountant in the seat opposite you on
the train has folded up his *Daily Telegraph* preparatory to
getting off at Stockport. You forget immediately. Egnaro –
in the beginning, at least – hides itself in the interstices, the
empty moments of your life.

Lucas himself had a similar incidental quality. He was a
fattish, intelligent, curly-haired man, between thirty and
forty years old and prone to migraine headaches, who had
worked his way up from records and goldfish in the Shude
Hill Market to a shabby bookshop in one of the grim streets
behind Manchester library. I did his accounts once a month
in a filthy office he kept above the shop; afterwards he
would treat me to a Chinese meal and pay me in cash, for
which I was grateful. I sold some of my wife's books to him
when she died. He was quite decent to me on that occasion.

He conducted the business evasively. Receipts were
scribbled on decaying brown paper bags, in a variety of
hands. He had three signatures. I never knew how many
people he employed. He never paid his bills. He concealed
from me almost as much as he was concealing from his
suppliers, his partners, and his VAT inspector. To tell the
truth, I let him hide as much as he pleased: no one in the
grey streets outside cared, and I was glad of the work. I
hated the office, with its litter of half-empty plastic cups and
plates of congealed food; but I liked the shop. After the
rambling apologetic evasions upstairs it had a sour candour.

Its window was packed with colourful American comics
Sellotaped into plastic bags, and its door was always open.
Inside it was the relict of a dozen bankruptcy cases: car
rental, cheap shoes, do-it-yourself. Lucas had ripped out
the original fitments, leaving raw scars on the wall to remind
him, and replaced them with badly carpentered shelves. A
tape-player and two loudspeakers pumped the narrow
aisles full of a crude music which drew in the students and
teenagers who made up his bread-and-butter clientele.
They came in full of a sort of greedy idealism, to buy
science fiction and crank-cult material – books about

spoon-bending, flying saucers and spiritualism, books by Koestler and Crowley, Cowper Powys and Colin Wilson – all the paraphernalia of that 'new' paradigm which so attracts the young. As a sideline Lucas sold them second-hand records, posters, novelties, and – from a basement stinking of broken lavatories and mould – film magazines, biographies of James Dean, and children's comics.

They loved it. Every flat surface was strewn with the poor stuff they wanted, and I don't think that any of them ever realised that Lucas hated them, or that this was his revenge on them.

He kept the pornography at the rear of the shop. On slack afternoons he would stand beside the cash-desk, sealing the new stock into plastic wrappers so that the customers couldn't maul it. This activity seemed to relax him. His plump fingers had performed the task so often that they worked unsupervised, deftly folding the wrapper, pulling the Sellotape off the reel, smoothing it down, while Lucas's thoughts went elsewhere and his face took on a collapsed distant expression; so that he looked, with his curly hair and smooth skin, like a corrupt but puzzled cherub. Occasionally he would leaf through a copy of *Rustler* or *Big-Breasted Women in Real-Life Poses* before he sealed it up, or stare with sudden stony contempt at the businessmen browsing the back shelves.

Once or twice a month the police would come unannounced and remove his entire stock in black polythene dustbin-bags. No one expected this to have any effect. He had the shelves full again the next day. They treated him with a jocular familiarity, and in the face of their warrants and destruction orders he was resentful but polite. He made no distinction between pornography and science fiction, often wondering out loud why they confiscated the one and not the other.

'It all seems the same to me,' he maintained. 'Comfort and dreams. It all rots your brain.' Then, reflectively: 'Give them what they want and take the money.'

Though he believed his analogy, his cynicism wasn't as

simple as it seemed. The art student, with his baggy trousers and his magenta-dyed hair, coming in for the latest Carlos Castenada or John Cowper Powys; the shopgirl who asked in a distracted whine, 'Got anything about Elvis Presley? Any books? Badges?'; the accounts executive in the three-piece suit who snapped back his cuff to consult his digital watch before folding the new issue of *Young Girls in Full Colour* or *Omni* into his plastic attaché case – I soon saw Lucas's contempt for them stemmed from his fellow-feeling.

In unguarded moments he showed me some of his own collection: florid volumes illustrated in the twenties and thirties by Harry Clark; Beardsley prints and Burne-Jones reproductions. He had newspapers from the fifties and sixties, announcing the deaths of politicians and pop stars; he had original recordings by Jerry Lee Lewis and Chuck Berry. If he knew exactly what the teenagers wanted to buy, it was because he was privy to their dreams; it was because he had haunted the backstreets of London and Manchester and Liverpool only a few years before, searching for a biography of Mervyn Peake, a forgotten novel, a bootleg record. And, if he hated them, it was because he had lost their simplicity, their ability to be comforted, the ease with which they consummated their desires.

He was trapped between the fantasy on the shelves, which no longer satisfied him, and the meaningless sheaves of invoices floating in pools of cold coffee on the desk upstairs. Therein lay his susceptibility to Egnaro. Where my own lay I am not half so sure.

'We all love a mysterious country,' said Lucas.

We were sitting in his office, looking through his collection, warming our hands over the one-bar fire which drew a sour failed smell from the piles of ancient magazines and overflowing waste-bins. The accounts for February were finished. His takings were down, he claimed, his overheads up. All that month a wind from Siberia had been depressing the city-centre, scouring Deansgate from the cathedral eastward, and forcing its way into the shops. Downstairs the tape-player was broken. Students drifted listlessly past in ones or twos, or clustered round the window with their collars turned up, arguing over the value of the cheap stuff inside.

'For instance,' Lucas explained, leaning over my shoulder to turn a page, 'this tribe has lived for centuries under a volcano on an island somewhere off the south-west coast of Africa. The exact latitude is unknown. The elders worship the volcano as a god; they're said to have inhuman powers.' He turned several pages at once, his pudgy fingers nimble. 'It's the draughtsmanship I love. There! You can see every head under the water, even the straws they're breathing through. Look at that stipple! You won't find drawing like that in the rubbish downstairs.'

He sighed.

'I used to spend hours with this stuff as a kid. See the spider monkeys, trapped in the burning village? They act as the eyes of the witchdoctor: he never sees anything for the rest of his life but flames!'

He had been preoccupied all day, sometimes depressed and edgy, at other times full of the odd nostalgic eagerness which with him stood in for gaiety. He couldn't settle to anything. Now he was showing me an illustrated omnibus of some American writer popular in the 1920s – Edgar Rice Burroughs or Abraham Merrit – which had cost him, he said, over a hundred pounds. It had been privately printed a decade ago and was very hard to come by. I could make little of it, and was surprised to find he kept it with his treasured editions of *Under the Hill* and *Salome*. The pictures seemed badly drawn and drab, unwittingly comic in their portrayal of albino gorillas and wide-eyed frightened women; the tales themselves fragmentary, motiveless and unreal.

'I've never seen much of it,' I admitted.

Personally, I told him, I had adored Kipling at that age. (Even now, if I close my eyes, I can still picture the Cat Who Walked Alone, his tail stuck up in the air like a brush and

that poor little mouse speared on the end of his sword.)
When he didn't respond I closed the book with exaggerated
care.

'It's very nice,' I said, 'but not my sort of thing. Are you
hungry yet?'

But he was staring down into the cold black street.

'It's almost as if he'd been there, don't you think?' he
said. 'Watching the way the ash drifts down endlessly over
the pumice terraces.'

He was talking to himself, but he couldn't do it alone. He
was trying to woo me, even though we had so little in
common he didn't know what to say. His obsession had
him by the throat, and the Rice Burroughs volume had only
been an introduction, a way of preparing me. Later I would
begin to recognise these moods, and learn how to respond
to them. Now I merely watched while he shook his head
absently, abandoned the window and, breathing heavily
through his mouth, made a pretence of fumbling through
the heaps of stuff under the desk. The book he came up with
fell open, from long usage, at a page about half-way
through. I see now that this is what he had wanted to show
me all along. He looked at it for a minute, his lips moving
slightly as he scanned the text, then nodded to himself and
thrust it into my hands.

'I always wondered what this meant,' he said, with a
peculiar deprecatory shrug. 'You might be interested in it:
what he really meant by it.'

It was an American paperback, one of those with the
edges of the pages dyed a dull red and the paper that smells
faintly of excrement. There were newer editions of it in the
shop downstairs; in fact it was quite popular. Its author
claimed to link certain astronomical events with the activi-
ties of various secret societies and Gnostic sects, although
what he hoped to prove by this was unclear. It was called
The Castles of the Kings, or something similar. The bookstalls
have been full of this sort of thing for the last ten years; but
Lucas's copy had been bought in the mid-fifties when it was
not so common, and its pages were tobacco brown with age.

While I was reading it he fussed round the office, shuffling through the invoices, trying to tidy the desk, warming his hands at the fire; but I could feel him watching me intently.

'We know what we see,' the passage began, 'or think we do. . . .' And it went on:

> . . . but is it possible that the real pattern of life is not in the least apparent but, rather, lurks beneath the surface of things, half-hidden and only apparent in certain rare lights, and then only to the prepared eye? A secret country, a place behind the places we know, which seems to have but little connection to the obvious schemes of the universe?
>
> In certain lights and at certain seasons the inhabitants of any city can see enormous faces hanging in the air, or words of fire. Also, one house in an otherwise dark street will be seen to be lit up at night for a week, even though no one lives there. From it will come sounds of revelry, although no one is observed to enter or leave it. Suddenly all is quiet and dark again, as if nothing had happened! But ordinary people will remember.
>
> Scientists give us many explanations to choose from. Are we really to believe that reality is built from tiny motes whirling invisibly about one another?

There was more of this; an account of an eclipse witnessed in China during the fourteenth century; and then the following curious paragraph:

> In India newly married couples wade in the estuarine mud catching fish in a new garment. 'What do you see?' their friends call from the bank. 'Sons and cattle!' is the answer. Are we to doubt that India exists? In the Dark Ages they had never heard of America! When the Jew of Tunis exhibited a fish's tail on a cushion, did anyone doubt that it was a fish?

'I don't quite see what he's getting at,' I said.

'Ah,' said Lucas. He thought for a moment. He had expected my reaction, I could see, but was disappointed all the same. 'You saw the hole in his argument, though?' He took the book gently from my hands and returned it to its heap. 'You saw through that?'

'Oh, yes,' I said, as positively as I could. 'I saw that.'

But he seemed dissatisfied. He stared at me for some time as if I had tried to mislead him over something obvious – the time of a train, say, or the name of a popular actress. I put my coat on under his watery blue-eyed gaze and we went out of the office in silence. It occurred to me suddenly that he saw no flaw at all in that 'argument', such as it was; and I wondered briefly how many casual acquaintances like my-self had been invited up to the office to puzzle over *The Castles of the Kings*, and how many more he had lent it to, in the hope that they would see what he saw in its skeins of unoriginal rhetoric and curious misinterpretations of the world.

Downstairs he looked round the shop with dislike, pocketed the take – perhaps eighty pounds – after a short discussion with the bored lad behind the cash-desk, and locked up. As we stood on the doorstep, fastening our coats against the scatter of snow coming down on the black Manchester air, he turned to me and dismissed it all with, 'Good for a laugh, though, that passage? Good for a laugh, anyway!' And I had the feeling he'd said that many times, too. 'By the way,' he went on, in the same dismissive tone, 'have you heard of this place they call "Egnaro"?'

'That's the Javanese place in Cross Street, isn't it?' I said. I thought perhaps he was bored with Chinese food. 'Would you like to try it tonight instead of the Lucky Lotus? We could easily go there.'

He looked at me as if this was the last answer in the world he had been expecting, then gave a queasy, almost placa-tory laugh.

'Easily go there!' he said, and took my arm.

Egnaro. It was a word, I found, that came easily to the tongue.

'Do you ever think', said Lucas later, prodding his chicken curry, 'that the only part of your life that really mattered is over?' And without giving me a chance to answer: 'I do.'

We were sitting in the Lucky Lotus, listening to the wet raincoats dripping in the alcove behind us.

'No, don't laugh,' he said. 'I'm serious. Once your childhood's over up here, they put you in the toothpaste factory. You get a council house in Blakely. You get piles, and watch "Coronation Street" for the rest of your life.'

He ate in the Lotus two or three times a week, mostly on his own, because it saved him the trouble of cooking for himself when he got home. The little Malay waitresses, I think, realised he was lonely, and surrounded him as soon as he sat down, joking about the weather in their gluey inexplicable accents. They had made of him a fixture, a fetish; and the Lotus, with its hideous maroon flock wallpaper, dirty tablecloths and congealed rice, seemed like a natural extension of the office in Peter Street. He ate his food with a sort of lugubrious greed, planting his elbows firmly on the table before he began, eyeing his plate suspiciously, and surrounding it with his forearms as if he thought someone might take it away before he had finished.

'That hasn't happened to you,' I pointed out. 'You've got the shop. You've chosen a different kind of life.'

He stared for a long time at a piece of meat on the end of his fork. 'You never escape,' he said finally. Then: 'Look, I don't want to put you off, but could you just smell this?' He waved the fork under my nose. 'It tastes a bit funny.'

He had been in a curiously self-pitying state since showing me *The Castles of the Kings*. I suspect that he regretted revealing even this small corner of his private life. We make ourselves vulnerable with confidences. But, whether this was so or not, now he had broached the subject he was unable to leave it alone. I had an uneasy impression that he was approaching some sort of crisis. He had drunk a lot of lager with the barbecued spare ribs, but I could see that it had given him little relief from whatever was worrying him. After I had reassured him about the chicken, which seemed perfectly all right to me, he said: 'I used to think: What if the maps were all wrong and the world was full of undiscovered countries! Undiscovered countries! What a joke.'

His jaws moved slowly from side to side; then he shook his head, swallowed, and pushed his plate away.

'It was too late even then. The world was full of housing estates.' He stared into the distance. 'The twenties and thirties – that was the time to be young. You could still have believed they'd made a mistake then.'

While I was thinking about this a waitress came up and asked, 'Dya wa' so' costa' na'?'

'What?' I said.

She giggled.

'Wan' costa'? Rass pa'?'

'Oh, yes,' said Lucas. 'Custard and rice pud.' He nodded vigorously at her. 'I've been having that all week,' he explained to me. 'They soon get used to your habits here. Sometimes I can't understand a word they say. I think that's why I come.'

She brought him his sweet.

'As a kid (and you'll laugh at this, I warn you),' he said, 'I used to believe that I'd been born on some unknown continent and brought here by slavers. When I shut my eyes at night I could hear voices like hers, above the sound of the breakers on some rotting beach. It was the most frightening country in the world. The river deltas were full of radioactive silt. The natives mined a kind of green gold. They were beautiful – almost white, very intelligent, very tall and kind. It was somewhere in the Antarctic.'

He put down his spoon and stared around. He gulped suddenly.

'Christ,' he whispered. 'I'd still rather be there than here!' And he looked quickly down into the sticky mess on his plate.

I didn't quite know what to say.

'I'm sure we all feel like that sometimes,' I tried. 'But isn't it escapism? Perhaps the housing estates are the real undiscovered countries—'

He gave me a look of contempt.

'Very clever. You've never lived on one of the fuckers.'

He was silent for a long time after that. The place had been full of clerks and secretaries having their dinner before they went to the cinema round the corner in Deansgate, the women in their winter boots, the men in their three-piece suits. Now it emptied itself steadily, marooning me with him. The manager, who spoke no English though his arithmetic was perfect, came out from behind the bar; and, with the girls clustered twittering around him, began some sort of game at a vacant table. Lucas stirred his pudding round in its thick white dish until it was cold, taking small sips of the sticky coffee-flavoured liqueur he had ordered earlier. I bit my lip and concentrated on the wall, embarrassed. Suddenly he looked up again. Tears were running down his cheeks.

'Are you sure you've heard nothing about Egnaro?' he said.

'The thing is', he continued, before I could say anything, 'that I've just about convinced myself a place like that exists.' He rubbed his eyes with the back of his hand. 'I'm sorry. It's that I get the feeling everyone else knows, you see; and they aren't telling me.' He laughed. 'Stupid, isn't it? I suppose we all get stupid ideas.' He got up and pulled a roll of dirty five-pound notes from his pocket. 'Will twenty quid do you this month? I'm a bit short at the moment. You know how it is. I'll get the bill.'

I made him sit down and drink a cup of coffee. I made him tell me about Egnaro, and now I wish more than anything else in the world that I hadn't.

The dead miners of Egnaro lie looking up at the sun, the blackness of their flesh tarring the long bones. A gull spreadeagles itself on the air above them; a hot wind blows along the shore, peeling off a few flakes of gold leaf that still cling to their darkened skin. Egnaro! It is a dangerous place, which steals over you like a dream. It is the name of your most basic questions about the universe; it is the funnel-tip from which your life fans back. All myths are perversions of its history; it is the secret behind the apparent history of the world. It is at once inside and outside you, and it signals all men at some time in their lives, like a flare of electricity along their nerves. It is as simple as a conversation half-heard on top of a bus. . . .

'A woman sitting near me spoke to her neighbour. It was my stop. The bus gave a lurch and I had to get off. Standing there on the pavement in the rain I realised she had said: "Egnaro, where they have so many more senses to choose from!" I knew immediately I had misheard her. I laughed and walked off. But I recalled it later, and it has come to haunt me.'

This was how Lucas began his explanation, under the dripping raincoats in the Lucky Lotus that evening at the end of February. I had to prompt him to begin with. (Had he, for instance, heard the other woman's reply? It turned out he hadn't.) But as his confidence grew, though he was often confused and incoherent, he seemed to exchange his self-pity for a kind of puzzled wonder: his eyes took on a watery glint of enthusiasm, his speech a crude lyrical quality. He spoke for a long time. Couples came in, ate under the dim lights, and went out again. The waitresses eyed us benignly and giggled. After all, he was a fixture there. Would he like some more costa'?

' "Egnaro, where they have so many more senses to choose from!" '

From the moment he heard that meaningless half-sentence, a kind of dam seems to have burst in his brain. 'It was like rubbing condensation off a window pane and looking out at a landscape you don't understand.' He was inundated by hints and clues, often of the slenderest nature. In an issue of the *Sunday Times* Business News he had picked up from the floor of a train he read: 'Exploration budget cutbacks could still stall our industrial recovery.' He knew exactly what he was supposed to gather from that, but he couldn't say how. In two critical lines of Louis Mac-Niece's 'Streets of Laredo' he discovered this misprint: ' "Egnaro the golden is fallen, is fallen;/Your flame shall not quench nor your thirst shall not slake." ' It was someone else's copy of the book. And once, sheltering from a thunderstorm in the doorway of Tesco's, he had this bizarre experience.

The lightning flickered like a broken fluorescent lamp. Between flashes the sky was dim and greasy. The porch began to fill up with cripples also sheltering from the rain. 'Every poor handicapped bastard in Blakely seemed to have ended up in that porch.' They had been gathered in, Lucas felt, not by the wind and the rain, but by omens and premonitions experienced that morning in front of the gas-stove. They came prodded by 'instincts that last meant something when we were all frogs'. There were old ladies with blasted arthritic fingers and great varicose carbuncles; a tall man staring at the shiny stump of his left arm and singing hymns; a girl with a deformed lip and leg-irons. There was a very small woman with a hump on her back. 'You felt', Lucas said, 'that if you asked them why they'd come here the answer would be: "My dog spoke to me of Egnaro, the queer old thing, and I came"; or "I heard we would all be cured there". I felt that very strongly.' But they only looked at him; and, when the rain had stopped, left him there with his shoes full of water. 'None of them actually spoke.'

Thus Egnaro simultaneously hid from and revealed itself to him; in obliquities. 'It was impossible to verify anything,' he complained. 'The taxi was always driving away from me; by the time I looked up it had gone. I always found I'd used the newspaper to light the fire. People took back books I hadn't finished reading.'

He searched through all the atlases and encyclopedias he could find, but discovered nothing (although once, in *Baedeker's Northern Italy*, he came upon a typographical error which looked like 'Ignar' or 'Ignari'; it was on a map of

Livorno, near the new port). Nothing was made public, but by now he could hear the conspiracy all around him. It made an expectant sound, he said, like people filing into a cathedral or an empty concert-hall. It had affected the economy of the country, he believed; it had soured and complicated international relations. Fleets were outfitting on both sides of the Atlantic, in the Channel, the Baltic, and all along the Mediterranean seaboard, in a race to exploit the new country. Whoever got there first would reap enormous wealth from its mineral resources, the new science of its mysterious inhabitants, its incredible new animals; besides an immense strategic advantage. As soon as its exact whereabouts were known they would put to sea. Although this secret was jealously guarded, preparations so massive were necessarily known to many; ordinary people had been quick to pick up the rumour.

'They discuss it as a place to go for their *holidays*!' said Lucas in tired disgust. 'Will it be cheaper than Majorca? Its beaches less crowded than the Costa Blanca?'

('Costa'? Costa'?')

Suddenly we were back at the beginning. His face had collapsed into self-pity again and he had buried his head in his hands.

'Don't you see?' he appealed. 'If I don't find something out soon, they'll get there before me!' His shoulders shook. 'That's the real of horror of it, don't you see? If there really is such a place, then by the time *I* get there it'll be just the same as it is here!'

And he stared miserably at the maroon flock walls of the Lucky Lotus, the tears streaming down his cheeks again.

What could I do? I was appalled by his condition. And yet what he had said did not really touch me. I had always rather admired his cynical resilience; I couldn't begin to imagine as yet the state he had got himself into. I remember thinking: How can anyone have become so desperately lost? But that may have been much later; and, besides, we never quite know what we mean by thoughts like that. Somehow I got him to cheer up and pay the bill. It was nine or ten o' clock at night by now. The waitresses fussed round him, but he didn't seem to notice them. He forgot his briefcase and they came running out after us with it. He thanked them absently. All it ever had in it was an old copy of *Rustler* and some broken pencils. When we emerged into the deathly quiet streets behind Deansgate he said he'd walk up to the cab-rank in St Peter's Square. I went with him that far but I couldn't wait.

'You'll be all right?' I asked him.

'Oh, yes,' he said. 'I've just got a bit of a headache now. I'll have a couple of Veganin at home. They'll get me off to sleep.' He got hold of my arm. 'It's just a silly idea, all this, you know. I'll get over it.'

There he stood, looking battered and out of place in the February wind, his loneliness outlined by the great doorway of the Midland Hotel behind him. There didn't seem to be many taxis about.

The city-centre was slow to recover from that winter. March was bitter; late snow in April flattened the daffodils and filled the gutters with brown slush; Easter came early but did nothing to help trade. People were reluctant to come out in the sharp unseasonable winds; they had no money when they did. Turnover fell in all the luxury shops and most of the supermarkets. Deansgate took on a deserted shabby appearance. You could find a few office workers hurrying out at lunchtime, but they were avoiding the pedestrian arcades of King Street where the spring fashions made colourful but somehow remote displays behind the plate-glass windows. The sandwich-bars were empty. How much of Lucas's failure was part of this wider picture, how much his own fault, is hard to say.

Towards the end of March, government waste committees threatened to cut the student grant for the third time in twelve months. (A few puzzled protesters marched down Peter Street with placards and a petition, only to drift off aimlessly when they reached the Square.) Shortly afterwards Lucas fell out with his main paperback suppliers, who were justifiably sick of him not paying his bills. Then, as the students trickled back and trade picked up, a series of leading articles devoted to 'these brokers of porn and purveyors of filth' appeared in the *Evening News*; and for a while the shelves at the back of the shop were raided almost every afternoon. This made Lucas's staff nervous and edgy: they ran out of false names to give the police and, tiring of Lucas's promises to have the tape-player mended, left him one by one.

Throughout this period he was preoccupied and indecisive. He fobbed his creditors off with increasingly dull excuses; absentmindedly signed his own name on agreements he could not hope to keep; and, whenever he could find someone to look after the shop for him, sat upstairs trying to control his headaches with handfuls of Veganin.

'You'd better start coming twice a month,' he told me, sensing that someone had to keep track of his called-in loans, convoluted trade-offs and trails of broken promises.

'Why don't we work out a system for you?' I suggested, but he couldn't follow it, and he never wrote anything down now, anyway. The take went straight into his trouser pocket at the end of each day and he paid off his bills in cash instalments, twenty or thirty pounds at a time. When I complained that the VAT people weren't happy with his figures he asked pettishly, 'What sort of figures do they *want*? Surely that's your job!'

'I won't just make things up,' I warned him, and he shrugged. It was an argument we had been through before. 'Everyone's corrupt,' he said. 'In the end.' I couldn't tell if it was a statement or a prediction. A worse row blew up between us in mid-April, when I found among his 'accounts' a bit of paper on which he'd written: *Egnaro! My heart yearns for some sight of your cloud-capped cliffs!* It was hard to read the rest, which had something to do with an oil-rig disaster and a 'secret' television play.

'I thought you'd got over this,' I said, as lightly as I could. 'I'm not sure what George will make of it.' George Labrom was the Customs and Excise inspector. We were expecting him that afternoon. I knew him slightly: he was a decent, even indulgent man, but he disliked Lucas, and his patience was diminishing. 'Still, if you want me to, I'll try and fit it in somewhere. . . .'

But Lucas wouldn't let me make a joke of it. He bit his lip, sighed heavily, and went over to the window where it would be easier to ignore me.

'Come on, Lucas,' I said angrily. 'Don't make me do all the work.'

He shrugged.

'You never "get over it",' he whispered. 'I thought you understood that. It never lets you go.' Then he laughed sourly. 'What use is all this, anyway? I'd rather have Egnaro than bloody George Labrom. If you don't want to help me—'

'I can't help you if you won't help yourself,' I pointed out.

'Fuck off, then, if that's your attitude.'

And we faced one another across the desk, the litter of unpaid bills and falsified invoices stretching between us like a paper continent neither of us remembered how to cross. After that I got used to his silences as I had got used to the smell of his waste-bin. Every fortnight when I pushed open the office door I would find him staring out of the window at the pedestrians below. 'Christ, how I hate those bastards!' he would say, apropos of nothing; or, pushing out his lower lip petulantly, complain about the headaches that stopped him from sleeping. 'I had a sickener last night. A real sickener.' I caught him pasting press-cuttings into a series of scrapbooks he had kept since he was fourteen – recording with a kind of morose glee the bankruptcies and deaths of the fifties pop stars who had been his adolescent heroes.

In his absence (for it was an absence, as I now know from experience, even if he sat there all day) someone broke the shop window and stole most of the more valuable comics; he had allowed the insurance to lapse, and the window was never properly reglazed. Inside he put up notices saying, *We do not want people reading these magazines if they have no intentions of buying!* but by now his stock was so old that even the businessmen had abandoned the back shelves. (They were the last to go: years afterwards, you felt, they would still be wandering hopefully along Peter Street in their lunch-hour, like animals searching for a lost waterhole.) Once or twice I sat behind the desk myself, putting books in bags under the dusty flickering strip-lights. It was a novelty at first, but the cold cavernous silence, the filthy blue carpets, and the innuendos of the debt-collectors soon frightened me off. One Tuesday morning in May I had the bailiffs in, two heavily built men in sheepskin car-coats who knew Lucas of old.

They leafed through old issues of *Cockade* while they waited for him to turn up with his last quarter's rent. It was, they said, a month overdue. When he arrived he was smiling, puffed, red in the face, the jacket of his safari suit flapping open as if he had been running all over the city since eight o' clock in the morning. 'Oh, hello, gents,' he said. 'If you'd given me a bit more time. . . . Still, I've got just under half of it here, and I'm off for the rest now.' In fact he only had a third, and when he came back again he had nothing at all, so they took his keys, locked the shop up, and over the next few days sold off the remaining stock by auction. It went for an average of ten pence a book, I believe, and certainly didn't fetch enough for the rent.

Included among all the bales of *Count*, *Peaches* and *Chariots of the Gods* was Lucas's collection from the upper room: every one of his Beardsleys, Harry Clarks, first editions of Ishmael Reed.

He wanted to try to buy some of the stuff back, so I went with him to the auction. It was a dismal affair conducted in a large empty Edwardian room. A lot of his competitors were there, nodding to him nervously as they bought up his assets, hoping he wouldn't commit suicide in the lavatories and wondering who would 'go bump' next. He hardly bought anything. *Lysistrata* had gone at the beginning, stuffed in among a bunch of old science fiction magazines. He seemed stunned that no one there could tell the difference. 'They can't even bloody pronounce it,' he kept saying. 'The bastards!' He drank a lot at lunch-time and began to complain of a headache. He seemed reluctant to be on his own and in the afternoon insisted we go to the cinema, where we watched uncomprehendingly some sort of comedy. The flickering of the screen made his migraine worse, and when we came out he was blinking and shaking his head.

'What will you do now?' I asked him.

'I don't know,' he said irritably. 'Go home and watch "Crossroads", I suppose. What else is there?'

It was the rush-hour. As we pushed our way through the pedestrians the traffic was beginning to congeal at the junction of Peter Street and Deansgate, where no one ever obeys the traffic-lights. Lucas turned down towards the shop. He had spotted quite a large crowd of students and children gathered in front of the cracked window. They seemed to be waiting for the door to open. The younger ones kept trying it, rattling the handle then pressing their noses to the plate glass; they peered into the gloomy depths of the place, where they could just make out looming empty shelves and torn posters. The students, meanwhile, leaned against the wall with their hands in their pockets; and it was one of them who got up the courage to approach us, unzipping a plastic holdall.

'Want to buy some records?' he asked in a slow voice. He offered the open bag for inspection. This seemed to incense Lucas, who blinked and rubbed his forehead wildly.

'It's closed down, you stupid bugger!' he shouted. 'Can't you see?'

The rest of them turned slowly, like cattle interrupted drinking, and stared at him.

'Closed! Finished! Understand? You won't be getting any more of that here!'

He laughed. He swayed.

'What's the matter, Lucas?' I said. 'Come away!'

He pushed at me.

'Leave me alone. I'm all right,' he said. In a quieter voice he advised the crowd, 'Piss off and find someone else.' They watched him stagger off down Peter Street towards

the Midland Hotel, their eyes uncommunicative and in-
turned. Some of the younger ones laughed or catcalled
uncertainly. He was obviously in difficulties. He kept stop-
ping, holding his head, looking round as if he wondered
where he was. I went after him. Suddenly he wobbled to the
edge of the pavement, got down on his knees, and began to
vomit almost carefully into the gutter. People from the
bus-queues on the steps of the Free Trade Hall moved
hesitatingly towards him. He looked lonely and embarrassed, wiping his mouth with his handkerchief, blinking
and grinning up into the light that was causing him so much
pain. 'What can I do, Lucas?' I said. 'What's wrong?'

'Just piss off.'

Twenty or thirty people now surrounded us. At the front
stood the women from the bus-stop, clutching their shop-
ping-bags and umbrellas, a ring of greyish anxious faces.
Behind them men from the car showrooms and drawing-
offices struggled quietly for a better view. What was the
matter? It was a car accident. It was two men fighting. A
woman had fainted. It was a dog. Lucas squirmed about,
moaning with pain, squinting up at them as they discussed
him, screwing up the flesh round his eyes against the mi-
grainous coronal light that flared round their heads. Then,
quite suddenly, the headache seemed to leave him. He
shoved me away and jumped lightly to his feet. He looked
more relaxed and healthy than I had ever seen him.

'What do *you* know of Egnaro?' he demanded in a loud
and scornful voice.

Surprised and puzzled, the crowd drew back from him.
This seemed to amuse him. He laughed, and spat in the
gutter.

'What will you *ever* know?' he pressed them.

Some of them shook their heads. He winked horribly at
the women, grinned at the men. They backed off farther,
but he had their attention.

'You', he went on, 'with your supermarket tunes and
your Wimpey houses! You with your *insurance policies*!'

He darted forward, ransacked briefly some woman's

shopping while she stared helplessly on, and held up a packet of Daz. 'You', he accused her triumphantly, 'with your "blue whitener"!'

He sneered at them; he imitated their favourite television personalities; his effect on them was astonishing.

'If you want to know about the Golden Land,' he challenged them, 'you must *go there*!' The schoolchildren worked their way forward through the crush and gazed up at him. He regarded them indulgently. 'You must suffer as I have', he told them, 'in its swamps! You must itch with its fevers and yellow rashes, tremble on its lee shores, wade through its foetid deltas until your feet rot on your legs!'

The children cheered.

Lucas shook his finger in admonition. He put his hands on his hips.

'I know you!' he cried. 'You whisper that word among yourselves when you think I can't hear! But dare you speak it aloud? Dare you?'

I hadn't any idea what to do for him. In the end I abandoned him there with his puzzled but enchanted audience: a fat latter-day Errol Flynn or Mario Lanza, recruiting for some trumpery desperate expedition against the Incas among the crumbling jungles of Hollywood's 'new' world. His eyes were flashing, his curly hair was plastered to his forehead, he had gone insane. As I walked off I thought: He's spent his life exploiting their fantasies to subsidise his own. This is his punishment. I was quite wrong.

'That place is not for you!' I heard him cry, and they groaned. 'That place is for dreamers!'

One word hung in the air above him, heavy with promise yet bubbling and buoyant, a marvellous word sparkling with mystery and force; he had only to open his mouth and it would speak itself. A policeman was approaching the crowd from the direction of St Peter's Square.

That was four months ago. I did not see Lucas again until yesterday, although for a while I made regular visits to Peter Street, hoping he might be drawn back to the scene of his

failure. What I expected of him I don't know: that he should
recover from his breakdown, I suppose, and begin again.
He had, after all, paid me in cash. I imagined him in the
dirty streets behind Woolworth's or the Arndale Centre,
trying to raise finance among the market-stalls and pet-
shops where he had begun his career, two patches of black
sweat growing steadily under the arms of his safari suit as
his peculiar splay-footed walk carried him from disappointment to disappointment. But the place remained deserted
(it was to reopen much later as an extension of Halfords'
already profitable bicycle department); Lucas seemed to
vanish into his own fiction; and all I could do was stare at
my own reflection in the cracked plate glass.

At about this time I began to have my own intimations of
Egnaro.

There was nothing original about my seduction; it was
dismally similar to Lucas's own, except that it began with a
dream.

I was standing in a high narrow room with white walls. It
was very hot; but in through the room's single window
came the sound of trickling water, and those scents which
water draws from dry vegetation. There was a thin thread of
music, one figure repeated over and over again on some
stringed instrument. I went to the window but the view was
blocked by a tree. All I could see through its shiny fat leaves
was a blur of sunlight. Where a ray of light penetrated this
curious foliage, it filled the room with a dusty glow the
colour of rose petals; from this I deduced that the sun was
sinking. Standing in that room, soothed by its proportions,
although I knew I was in some country so foreign I could not
imagine it, hearing that string-figure endlessly repeated, I
felt assuaged and yet excited, as if by a premonition of
future happiness. I heard someone begin to say, 'Comfort
us now and in the hours of our deaths.'

When I woke, it was with an unbearable pang of nostalgia. Boarding the train at Stockport that morning, I heard a
woman say distinctly, 'The coast, they claim, is a must at
this time of year,' and I knew I was lost. Since then I have

kept a little notebook. The popular advertisements are full of clues. One shows a tiger running in slow motion across a heartbreaking landscape of sand dunes; another, for banking services, a horse splashing through shallows. I record them all.

Like Lucas I have ransacked the atlases and encyclopedias, finding nothing. Unlike him I have visited the great seaports: London, Glasgow, Liverpool. By Southampton Water I sat down and wept; the wind was full of the sound of foreign voices, the scent of foreign fruit; I was dizzy with expectation. But no great fleet is gathering. Nothing can be seen of the great preparations which haunted Lucas and which now haunt me. In the governmental buildings near St James's Park they look blankly at you if you mention Egnaro; in the offices of the Royal Geographical Society they can tell you nothing. And yet somewhere they are gutting the records of old expeditions; repairing ancient maps; cross-examining old sailors who – three days battered by ice and gales in 1942 under the Southern Cross, hunted by some lean German raider – saw, or only thought they saw, a smudge of land on a heaving horizon, a ripple of white ice cliffs out from which may flow that current of warm, fresh, mysterious water. . . .

I am able to see myself quite clearly on these useless journeys, these errands run on behalf of my own imagination; but I cannot stop, and I understand now why Lucas had such difficulty in describing his condition. It is like inhabiting two worlds at once.

As I take my first hesitant steps away from the seashore, setting out through the shattered limestone hinterlands into the deep interior of the mystery, I begin to feel a need for reassurance, for an exchange of maps and notes, for some dialogue with those who have made the journey before me. Yesterday, on an impulse, I went back to the Lucky Lotus, that staging-post or coaling-port on the way to Egnaro. I suppose I had known all along that I would find him there when I needed him. He was sitting at his table in the alcove, putting bits of sweet and sour pork into his mouth while he read the paper folded alongside his plate.

'Oh, hello,' he said. 'I was just thinking about you.' And when I had ordered my food he began talking about himself.

He had been to America, he said, since getting his affairs in order. If he was a bit fatter, that was why. New partners – he didn't want to be specific at this stage – had paid off most of his old debts, and he was ready to start a new business. America had opened his eyes. 'Fast food,' he said. 'That's where the real money is. Hamburgers. Bloody hell, you should see the way they do it over there!' It was like a production line. You took the customers' money, passed them through the system as quickly as possible, and ejected them at the other end. 'They hardly have time to get the muck down them before they're out on the street again and the next lot are coming in!' It was wonderful. 'Fast food, that's where it is.'

I watched him eat his rice pudding and custard, smacking his lips appreciatively, nodding and winking at the waitresses. I noticed that he had replaced his old leather briefcase with a brand-new plastic one. He used the word 'secret' constantly. 'The secret's in the condiments,' he would say. 'Give them onion relish and they'll eat anything.' And: 'In and out fast, that's the secret.' He had a second liqueur; he seemed quite willing to stay and talk. He asked me if I would like to get in on the ground floor of fast food with him, and I said I would. He didn't turn the conversation to old times, and I suspected he would have resisted me if I had. I sat listening to his new dreams, watching the hands of the clock.

'Well,' he said eventually. 'Time to push off, I suppose.'

I still had not brought myself to ask. I knew how he had felt every time he took out *The Castles of the Kings* and offered it to some puzzled travelling salesman. I watched the waitresses surround him, twittering 'Costa' costa' costa' ' like little drab birds, as he got up to go, and my tongue stuck to the roof of my mouth. He paid the bill with a credit card. We walked along Deansgate and down Peter Street towards the cab-rank outside the Midland Hotel. As we passed the shop, with its mended window and brand-new 'Halfords' sign, I managed to say: 'By the way. All that ''Egnaro'' stuff. . . .'

For a moment, he looked puzzled. Then he laughed. 'Oh, you don't have to worry about that,' he said, putting his hand on my shoulder. 'I've finished with all that. I can't think why I made so much fuss. It's nothing at all when you know, is it?'

I knew then that if I reached out I would touch some transparent membrane which had grown up between us to protect the secret. I nodded hopelessly. 'That's fine,' I said. 'Good.' I arranged to meet him again soon. I arranged to meet his backers. I walked away, and later caught my train. I shan't see him again. Old maps are useless.

I confess to you now as Lucas confessed to me under the coats in the Lucky Lotus last February – out of fear, out of puzzlement, out of loneliness.

Wherever I am I think about it, whatever I do is tainted by it, but if you were to ask me what Egnaro is I could give you no answer. In my most despairing moments I believe that the human race exists solely to give it expression. No one, I suspect, can have any clear understanding of it. All events are its signature; none is. It does not exist; yet it is quite real. The secret is meaningless before you know it; and, judging by what has happened to Lucas, worthless when you do. If Egnaro is the substrate of mystery which underlies all daily life, then the reciprocal of this is also true, and it is the exact dead point of ordinariness which lies beneath every mystery.

Birthday!

Fay Weldon

THEY met on their birthday, at a party, and discovered that they had been born on the same day twenty-eight years earlier. He in the morning, she in the evening. June 19th: Gemini: the Twins. Over the cusp and you were into Cancer, which meant you were home-loving, and Molly was, if anything, a little more home-loving than Mark, which was as it should be.

Molly and Mark. Two M's. M for mother, morality, meanness, martyrdom, mine. Except for mother, M isn't the warmest of initials but, then, mother makes up for a lot. Molly craved warmth, and enclosure and security, and acknowledgement; and Mark craved approval, and love. Well, everyone craves love. To love is almost more important than to be loved. Molly thought that; Mark tended to think the other way round. But, then, their natal moons were in different Houses – Molly's in the fourth, the House of the home, and Mark's in the tenth, the House of occupation. Molly's moon was in Capricorn and Mark's in Taurus. Capricorn is a rather sorrowful sign; Taurus just plain sexy.

Molly's mother and Mark's mother were both careful people and had kept an accurate note, in their respective diaries, of the hour of birth of their children. That was why both Molly and Mark could be so sure of their natures, as defined at any rate by astrologers – and the old-fashioned kind of astrologer, at that, who works out charts in detail and by tables, not the new-fashioned kind who uses a silicone-chip computer and disregards the moon. The moon is a strong influence on anyone's character, in particular anyone female, and should not be disregarded.

They were united in their dislike of their mothers. It was their unholy bond. They had never admitted it to anyone before. Oh, but it is the worst bond of all. If you are to love your life, you must love your mother. Somehow. It is the stuff from which you sprung. Deny the good in that and you deny the good of everything.

Mark's mother had grand relatives and a fluty voice and other sons who rose in the ranks of the Army and the Church and married nice young girls in churches full of flowers. Mark was expelled from school, failed to get to Sandhurst or even university, lived by odd carpentry jobs and married Molly, who was no one, in a registry office full of plastic roses. Mark's mother was there, but looked rather unhappy. Mark's father was in Uganda, as usual.

Molly's real father lived a bohemian kind of life with a famous lady artist on whose money he lived. Molly longed to be owned by them, but feared, rightly enough, that they found her boring. Nervousness in their company made her voice hard and her remarks edgy, and she knew she was never at her best when she was with them. Her father and stepmother had a row on the way to her wedding, and never got there. Their rows were like that – they would stop the traffic for miles around. Molly was relieved and aggrieved, all at once. Molly longed for Mark, and money. That's another M. Not much money.

Did they believe what they were saying, Mark and Molly, as they gazed into each other's eyes, in those first few months? Did they really see themselves written in the stars? Well, why not? They felt it. Love transmuted them: the base metal of reality turned to gold around them.

Perhaps it's better for a man and woman in love not to be the same age? Perhaps the old tradition, that a woman marries a man a few years older than herself, so that he is not just a little older but a little wiser than she, is in fact desirable? So that in every household in the land it can be perceived that the man rules, and the woman acquiesces, and that in this lies natural justice, richness, happiness and fruitfulness? They discussed this, too; and then they married. Of course.

Perhaps mothers who keep diaries and don't lose them are not the best mothers in the world? Molly's mother was a complainer. She had been left by her first husband, Molly's father, had a hard time bringing up Molly by herself, without support, had married again, and still complained, with reason, for her new husband was a mean and rigorous man, and would not give a penny to a starving cat, as Molly's mother put it.

Molly preferred not to think about money, but knew she needed it. Not much money. Just enough to live with a little warmth and peace and fitted carpets and curtains you could close against the world, keeping stress and anger and upset out, and love in. Not money for show or display, not for minks and gold taps; just money so you didn't have to snatch and save and think about it, or work out how the electricity was to be paid for, or even bother to remember when the bills fell due.

Mark liked money to spend; Mark liked money to be there, like magic. Mark believed everyone had money behind them, in securities, and before them, in legacies; and the fact that he had neither, because somehow the family fortune had been lost in Uganda, made no difference to the way he *felt* about money.

Molly had Jupiter in the second House, and Mark had Jupiter in the tenth House, which made money important in their lives. Molly's Jupiter was well aspected to the moon, Mark's badly. Molly was better with money.

They discussed all this in the first weeks of their marriage.

'We've got to start as we mean to go on,' said Molly, looking at the champagne on the bedside table, 'and we can't go on like this.'

Champagne went to her head, deliciously. Part of her loved parties, just as Mark did. Silken shifts and sparkling shoes and lovers' looks across the room. It was just, perhaps, that her natal moon had gazed down from Capricorn, three-quarters full, waxing, and clouds had scudded across it, and obscured its brightness.

Molly was a little taller than Mark, who was finely built and slidey-eyed, like a naughty faun. Molly's jaw was a little large and her nose a little long; she wished she had been born littler, less competent.

Her natal moon stared sideways and unsquarely at Saturn and made her practical.

'We can't go on like this,' she said.

'We won't,' he said. He loved her, his heavenly twin, his earthly mate. He wished he had been born on a bigger scale, more competent.

His natal moon went hand in hand with Venus; in collusion, as it were. It made him faithless.

'I'll always be true to you,' he said. 'This is all I require for ever and ever amen.' And he did not even cross his fingers as he spoke. Then.

Well. Mark threw away the champagne-bottles, found a job as a junior accounts executive in an advertising agency and took out a mortgage on a little house in the suburbs.

Molly took a part-time job as receptionist to a local dentist. The job was way beneath her capacity but about equivalent to her qualifications. Her schooling had been much disrupted, as her mother changed house and husbands, and no one at home had believed much in education. And the fact that she worked part-time enabled her to paint and polish the little house and cook Mark's dinner when he came home from work.

Molly learned to roof, and plumb, and wire, and carpenter. Someone had to. There seemed to be so very little money. Mark was only a junior executive in his advertising agency, earned just enough to keep things going, and came home tired and dispirited. And, in a way, having a house and a mortgage and a job and a future had been Molly's idea, not Mark's. Mark, she knew quite well, could have lived from hand to mouth on champagne for ever, not having a moon in Capricorn. So really, thought Molly, it was up to her to make a go of things.

'He should do more,' said Molly's mother, staring at her daughter's lime-chapped hands. Molly had been demolishing a plaster wall, breaking through the division between the two little ground-floor rooms, to make one large airy one, and the plaster was old, and lime-filled, and got in her hair and hands and clothes.

It was the kind of thing Molly's mother did say. Mark observed that Molly's mother just didn't like men. (Molly's mother had Mars in Taurus, badly aspected.)

'Mark works hard enough at the office, Mother,' said Molly. Mark's hands were smooth and pale and long-fingered, beautifully manicured. Molly loved them, outside and inside her body.

Molly was, increasingly, somehow workaday herself – she felt it. She read recipe-books and lit candles and created an atmosphere of romance, when she could. Mark liked that. It stopped him slumping in front of the television, which was an old man's trick, not a young one's.

'You can't mean to live here for ever,' complained Mark's mother. 'Supposing you had children!'

Through Mark's mother's eyes their street was mean and dingy, strewn with tattered papers and abandoned cars; a street no taxi-driver had ever heard of. (Mark's mother had Jupiter in mid-heaven. She lived grandly.) But Molly loved her house: her little suburban house. Mark came home to it.

Molly was a little vague about what happened at Mark's office. Mark put up with it for her sake; she knew that and was grateful. And Presentation Day happened about once every three months, and entailed late nights, exhaustion and worry. It was, apparently, when a new campaign was presented to a client, and was either accepted, which meant a bottle of champagne – reminiscent of other, carefree days – or rejected, which meant a stiff upper lip and a few sleepless nights, and try again. But Mark was very good.

He didn't bring his work home, either literally or spiritually, if he could possibly help it. That was how Molly liked it. There was the world outside the curtains, which was less and less to do with her, and the world inside, which was her kingdom, and Mark was its King.

The new baby had Aquarius rising, the sun in Libra, and the moon in the ninth. A happy, benign, kindly little soul. Her Saturn was in the fourth House, though, the House of the family, and badly aspected. Molly had, for the time, rather gone off astrology, and didn't give the matter much thought. Nappies and gas-boilers and feeds and pram-sheets are such practical things, making the stars in their courses seem irrelevant. A new mother with a new baby gets through her day as best she can. They called the baby Angela. Molly's stepmother, the painter, must have thought it was rather an ordinary name, for she forgot to send a card, let alone a gift, or money. Molly thought rather a lot about money, these days. Mark paid a sum into the joint account every month, but he had no idea of the reality of inflation, of course. Men didn't. And he had to look smart for work; he had to have silk ties and shirts with firm collars, and well-cut suits and hand-made shoes. Advertising was like that.

She gathered that Mark didn't like advertising. It seemed to him vaguely immoral. He found his colleagues phoney and tricksy, and prone to stabbing each other in the back. He bought sandwiches for lunch, he told Molly; and walked in the park and thought about nature, and the craft of the woodworker, and whether it wouldn't be possible for his little family, one day, if they could somehow save enough money, to live in the country, naturally, as God had meant man (and woman) to live.

Well, Mark's moon was strongly aspected to Neptune, which gave him a spiritual side to his nature. Molly's moon made no aspect to Neptune at all.

And how were they to save? Molly managed marvel-lously (three M's in a row; add Mark, and that makes four! Four square corners to a safe, secure world!), but money was so hard to come by. You can buy flaky soap cheap, and Molly did, but half a pound of butter is half a pound of butter, and costs what it does.

'It's the Common Market!' said Mark sadly. 'The international conglomerates have done it; it's they who've sent us on this helter-skelter inflationary slide. And to think I'm part of that kind of world! But what can I do?'

What indeed? It takes money to change jobs, and a man with a house, a wife and a family can't be irresponsible. Mark sopped up responsibility for Molly, stole light from her moon. It was marvellous. The M's kept coming.

So did the family. Within three years there were three little girls. Angela, Anthea, and – Molly's stepmother shrieked and said, 'No, not another A, not Annabel,' so they called her Bernice instead.

Angela, Anthea and Bernice. Anthea's sun was in Aries and Bernice's was in Taurus and all three were mid-signs, born respectively on the third, seventh and fifth of their months, which kept their characters distinct and unneurotic, and not cuspal. People born as sun-signs change – as were the parents Mark and Molly – can veer uneasily from one nature to another. The transition from Gemini to Cancer is not easy, Gemini being so very undomestic and Cancer so very home-based.

Mark fell in love with a girl called Stella from Market Research. She was a Virgo. 'By name but not nature,' as Mark said to Stella in bed. He told Molly that was what he said to her in bed, because he confessed everything to Molly, everything, after a secretary at the office, a girl called Amantha, a Sagittarian, had telephoned Molly to say Mark was having an affair with Stella. Why did Amantha make such a phone-call? Perhaps, Molly thought, because she was a Sagittarian and quick on the telephone and swift to intervene in the cause of natural justice.

Molly wept for days, and Mark tried to excuse himself for still more days. Or not so much to excuse, for these things happen, but to explain. Advertising was such a strange world, with strange values, and a strange language of its own, that he always felt ill at ease in it. He could not join in with the others, yet was doomed to live with them from ten to five every day. 'Or six, or seven, or eight, or even midnight,' mourned Molly. 'They work you so hard and pay you so little!'

She had forgiven him days ago. He could not forgive himself.

Their standards were not his, their world not his, he would explain, in the night hours when they lay awake, side by side. He belonged to Molly, and to Angela, Anthea and Bernice. They were *real*, as the world of advertising was not. It was just he had been away for the weekend at a Presentation and Stella had been there, and the hotel so bleak and unfriendly and he had missed his family so much.

'I understand, I understand,' said Molly. 'Let's just go to sleep. I have to get up at six.'

She did, too. She liked to spend her evenings with Mark, just sitting, while he recovered from his day, and that meant leaving the dinner dishes until morning; and, as she also liked him to have breakfast in a tidy house with his children, clean and orderly, about him, that meant getting up at six, even earlier. She was pleased enough to do it.

But Mark's moon was in conjunction with Mercury, and he did not stop explaining easily, once he had started, and in the mornings, long after the Stella episode had finished, she would be bleary-eyed and yawning.

But it had finished. Finally and for ever. Stella had moved to another agency. Sometimes the phone would ring and when she picked up the receiver no one answered, but why should that be Stella? These things did happen in a marriage. It happened all the time to Molly's mother, when living with Molly's father. Molly resolved that her marriage would be strengthened by this assault upon its integrity, and not weakened by it.

She resolved this, not merely for their own sake, but for that of Angela, Anthea and Bernice, and took care thereafter to be yet more loving, yet a better wife. But the episode with Stella had clouded Molly's happiness, dulled her eyes a little, as the clouds had dulled the moon at the time that she was born. Mark seemed as bright-eyed as ever. Well, that was how it went.

Molly had two terminations. There was not really the money for more children, or for the bigger house a larger family would demand. Molly and Mark talked about vasectomy, at the time that it was fashionable, but Molly thought she could not fancy a sterile man, and Mark said he'd be only too happy with a sterile woman, so Molly was sterilised. The sun was in opposition to the moon at the time, but the operation went well enough.

On their mutual birthday, every year, Mark took Molly out to dinner at a Chinese restaurant and told her how much he loved her. She adored the extravagance, and being waited upon, and impractical food you did not even have to finish, so as to be sure not to waste money. She was shocked, year by year, to see how the cost of restaurant meals soared. So, of course, did the cost of fish fingers and baked beans, which, over the years, and supplemented by vitamin tablets, seemed to be the staple diet of Angela, Anthea and Bernice. But all three had Capricorn stuffed with rich and benefic planets, so their lives could be expected to get better as they got older.

Every other year Mark would have to go off on a Presentation, or on a holiday cruise – for he was now account executive for a large travel agency and obliged to travel here and there; journeys from which he would return pale with exhaustion and overwork and fretted by the company of capitalists and idiots. It was a pity that his promotion coincided with the nation's economic recession, and that there was as little money as ever.

Time passed. Molly's parents no longer seemed to loom so large in her life as once they had done, and she was obviously of as little importance to them as ever. Her mother's complaints reeled faintly out into the heavens, and faded into nothingness somewhere out there amongst the stars. Her father no longer even bothered to send her a card at Christmas. Molly, if they remembered her, was someone from long ago, a gawky girl full of promise, who had long since come to nothing, lost in a suburban street in a world stuffed as full of suburbs as a haystack with straw. Molly no longer minded.

Then all of a sudden she and Mark were forty, and the girls were nine, eight, and six, and it was 20 June, the sun was passing from Gemini to Cancer, and three surprising things happened.

Mark gave her a video-cassette recorder for her birthday.

'It must have cost hundreds!' she breathed.

'It's from the office,' he said. 'All the executives have them now; even the junior ones like me. Well, there has to be some recompense for the life we lead. Some danger money for our souls!' And he gave her a bunch of red roses as well, in love and gratitude. The real present. Molly gave Mark, that morning, a book on pond life – for she had built a pond in the garden with her own hands, digging out and cementing and lining, so that Mark could put his tadpoles in it and grow frogs and feel nearer to the nature that he loved.

The second surprising thing was that Mark took the girls off to lunch at the office, so that she could have the day off, to do as she wanted. Wonderful! Well, he didn't take them actually into the office – not wanting, he said, to subject beings as tender and true as his daughters to the sordid glare of commercial life – but at least out to lunch at a French restaurant near the office. The girls usually came home for lunch, because school dinners had become so shockingly expensive.

The third surprising thing, even more surprising to Mark than to Molly, for he tried to eject them when they turned up, was a party from the office, who arrived in drunken hilarity, in three taxis, with champagne, to wish Mark a happy fortieth birthday, just as Mark and Molly were setting off for their Chinese restaurant.

Molly was quite excited. A party! She remembered thoughts of silken shifts and glittery shoes and lovers' glances across rooms, and realised how long it had been since they'd gone to a party, except up and down the street, where the dresses were Crimplene, the shoes came from

Marks & Spencer's, and no one looked lovingly, except perhaps the man from the television rental, who seemed to eye her sometimes with a fleeting nod and wink.

The girls clambered out of bed, the baby-sitter accepted champagne from the tooth-mug and a good time was had by all. Molly was amazed and gratified by how popular Mark seemed. How he underrates himself, she thought. And how well-heeled they look, she thought, and imagined that perhaps they regarded her shabby home askance.

Yet how could they? Why should they? She and Mark had what they could never have. If they looked, it was with envy. The malefics fighting in the sky: Mars and Saturn.

They had brought Mark a tribute, they said. A cassette to mark his birthday, made by his colleagues, starring his colleagues. Mark protested, but champagne and bonhomie drowned his protests, and the cassette was slotted into the new video, with its green digital clock and the two dots beating, beating life and time away.

'We made it in the TV Department,' they cried. 'Makes a change from blue films, any day.'

Molly shivered with shock. She could believe it of them, suddenly. Trendy, phoney people, after all, seeking amusement, pushing experience to its ultimate ends, coming slumming down in her nice homely house, intruding where they were not wanted, where they had not been asked. Blue films! And Mark had taken the girls near the place, and she had been glad, selfishly, wanting a day off, just one day.

And there the girls were on the film, staring at themselves out of the telly. Wouldn't they be spoilt? Surely it was bad for them? Didn't these people care? 'Happy birthday, Daddy!' Yet they seemed so sweet: hand in hand, little mid-cuspians, with their sturdy natures, and their afflicted fourth Houses. The House of the home.

But what was wrong with their home? Nothing. Astrology *must* be wrong. A false trail.

Then came a tribute from Mark's boss. The senior accounts executive. Red-faced, backed by a massive oil painting of ships at sea. He raised a glass to Mark. Was that the boardroom? It was *enormous*. Mark's boss was jovial and drunk.

'Are we on camera? Yes? From one king newt to another,' he said, 'here's wishing Mark may the next forty years be as lively as the last! The day he came on the Board was the day I should have handed in my notice, and I didn't, and I haven't looked back or, at any rate, up from under the table ever since! I daren't, because the Agency's gone from strength to strength and he's after my job. So here's to you, Mark, and may all your tots be doubles!'

The Board? Mark drinking? Mark never drank. He said it gave him a headache. He suffered from headaches in the morning, quite badly sometimes. And was somnolent in the evenings. But, then, many office workers were. Paperwork is a great strain, and dealing with people, and exercising judgements, and taking responsibility.

'Here's wishing you many happy returns, Mark,' said a gentle voice, and a simpering willowy blonde bit her lip and stared out of the camera, 'and this is the best present I can give you. Just a look.' And she edged away a corner of her blouse until a portion of white breast showed, which she rapidly re-covered, and the screen went blank and a great cheer went up from the audience.

'Put it away, Wendy! Put it away!'

Now another woman: older and darker and cleverer by far on the screen. Sleek and cross.

'Sod off, Mark,' she said. 'Even if you are forty, you can't expect pity from me. I may feel different by August, of course.' And the screen went blank and cries of 'Good for Stella!' went up, and somebody screeched: 'Stella always waits till the last minute before she changes her mind.' And somebody else said: 'But just don't tell Amantha!'

Stella? Stella was supposed to have moved to another agency years ago. August? August was when Mark had to go on the biannual fact-finding cruise which bored him so. Molly looked over to where Mark leaned against the sideboard – bought eight years ago from the junk-shop down the road. She thought he was avoiding her eye. Well, of course he was.

He was smiling, slightly, a strange, far-away, rueful smile. He is Gemini, she thought, all Gemini. Which twin are you kissing? The one who loves you or the one who doesn't? The one who needs you, or the one who keeps you in reserve? The one who comes home to you, the half-life, to rest while gathering strength for the real life, the true life, the office life: of girls and excitement and power and drink? Life, oh, life! Wife and children are the fail-safe net, just in case one day the good times stop. But why should they?

Someone else smiled from the screen now. A restaurateur. French. You could tell from the beret and the menu on the blackboard. Steak au poivre. £12.50. No, that must be a joke. Surely. That was the price of the whole birthday once-a-year celebration Chinese meal.

'Now from the lips of the man whom single-handed Mark has made rich,' sang the commentator, half on screen, half off it, for the cameraman seemed to be drunk, too, 'Monsieur Victor himself. Sing "Happy Birthday", Monsieur Victor.' Monsieur Victor shuffled and grinned and looked embarrassed and could not sing. 'Please,' begged the commentator, 'to the greatest gourmet of them all, to Mark, the man who loves smoked halibut by the pound, and Chablis by the crate! To Mark, on his fortieth birthday!' And the picture crumbled into confusion and laughter and suddenly a few of the guests were looking at Molly as if realising what they had done, and Molly was leaning against a wall, in the Indian caftan she had ironed and loved and looked forward to, and which now seemed absurd.

The television screen leaped into life again. Now it was a young man with a blonde moustache, raising a glass and saying, 'Until I met Mark I never knew that advertising and dirty weekends were synonymous, so happy birthday, Mark, King of the con-men,' and someone abruptly switched off the set and the party evaporated with nervous smiles and cries of, 'Surprise over,' and Mark and Molly were left together, with Angela, Anthea and Bernice, up far beyond their bedtime, flinging their arms around their father, crying, 'Happy birthday, Daddy! Happy birthday, Daddy dear. Oh, and Mummy, too, of course!

Christmas with a Stranger

Leslie Thomas

IT WAS Jones the Explosion, manager of the gas works at
Pontycan, who suggested that Caradoc should go to London for Christmas. The suggestion shocked a good many
people, Caradoc's mam for a start. It was not so much that
he was going away for Christmas – after all, he was thirty
now and no longer hung up his stocking. What upset her
was the spectre of London, a place, she believed, full of
shops and demons. People she had known in Pontycan
had gone there before, see, not only disappeared but
vanished. *Evangelists.*

But, argued Jones the Explosion, winking his one eye and
making surprisingly extravagant gestures with the stump of
his arm, the boy had the money now, so why shouldn't he
go? Pontycan was wonderful, but you had to see other
places, didn't you? Why, he himself had taken his con-
valescence at Weston-super-Mare.

There had, of course, been no shortage of suggestions of
how Caradoc should dispose of the money. Everybody
from Aneurin Howell, the *éminence grise* of Lipton's, to
Evans Above, who lived on top of the hill over Pontycan,
had plenty of ideas. A season ticket for Arms Park; a sly
week-end at Barry Island (with the woman of your choice); a
hundred Lipton Christmas hampers to be distributed to the
poor (Aneurin's brainwave); a new piano for his mam (a
suggestion from the neighbours).

Well, naturally, Caradoc bought his mam the piano and
there's pleased she was; she said she did not mind going to
Auntie Fan's for Christmas (the Auntie Fan, Bethelny Junction, that is), even though she found her sister's habit of
singing loudly in bed disturbing. Nor, incidentally, did she

like her making tea, for nocturnal consumption, in a hot-water bottle upon which she warmed her feet. But there it was, wasn't it?

On the day before Christmas Eve, Caradoc set out, smart in his suit and his dad's old watchchain, by railway from Pontycan to get the connection at Dinas Powis for Cardiff and onward to Didcot, Swindon, Reading and Paddington. What an occasion!

It was while he was on the train that the singular change came about. He was all right as far as Cardiff, for the landscape was chill and familiar. But the carriage was warm, and he enjoyed himself by, every now and then, touching his wallet. How lovely, thick with money.

No, it was after Cardiff that the transformation came about him. Once he had changed from the doddering valley-train to the fierce express that pushed its way, with massive confidence, over the mucky Usk at Newport and on to the foreign soil of England. It occurred all at once (later, describing it – in great confidence, of course – to Jones the Explosion, Caradoc used the expression 'in a flash', and Jones nodded understandingly). A wispy lady sitting opposite eyed his watchchain and asked the time. Caradoc pulled the chain from his waistcoat pocket, revealing it to be hanging empty as a dog's tail. Now, he knew perfectly well that his dad had only left him the chain, the watch having been disposed of during a hard fortnight. But now, to his own amazement, he heard himself saying: 'I'm afraid I lost the watch. In Madagascar.'

He was horrified at his own words. He felt as though someone else were telling the lie. The lady regarded the empty chain benignly, then said: 'Oh, Madagascar. There's nice.'

She said nothing until Swindon had steamed by and Didcot was approaching on clouds of rain. Then she leaned forward very kindly and enquired: 'Madagascar is foreign, isn't it?'

Unhappily Caradoc said: 'Yes, it's foreign. Ever so foreign.'

'And what were you doing in Madagascar?'

'Producing my latest film,' he heard himself saying with increasing horror and shame.

'Oh, there's nice,' she answered and, to his great relief, closed the subject for good. Guiltily Caradoc glanced around. A young lady in the far corner was smiling attractively towards him, and a pan-faced boy about twelve produced a piece of paper and asked for his autograph. Casting all conscience and caution away Caradoc wrote: 'Charles W. Ricks. Producer.' The boy read it and thanked him. The girl spread her teeth more beautifully. A smile seemed to grow within Caradoc also. He settled back and surveyed the wet Berkshire hills, trying to look as if he were searching for locations. By the time they had reached Paddington he was indeed Charles W. Ricks. He told the taxi driver so, and the man said he knew it, he recognised him from his photos in the newspapers. He asked to be taken to the Regent Hotel.

London and the Regent Hotel seemed to be the ultimate in grandeur. But Caradoc was not going to show it. Charles W. Ricks – producer of *Death in Madagascar*, *Train of Love* (an epic filmed entirely on the Cardiff–Paddington express) and (soon to be screened in London's West End) *Boncock*, the drama of a Cockey taxi-driver turned detective – surveyed all the glory with detachment.

He bought himself a fashionable shirt and a tie with a modest motif on it and some rather daring shoes. The only thing he failed to do was to alter his voice. When he told the hotel porter that he was from Hollywood, the man thought he said Holyhead.

Unfortunately, after almost a whole day and an evening, Charles W. Ricks turned out to be something Caradoc had never been – lonely. It was all very well walking about in his motifed tie and his smart shoes, but he realised that, for all its light and life, there was in the big city, even at Christmas, a remoteness that he had never known in the tight streets of Pontycan. In the hotel cocktail bar a man wished him a merry Christmas and asked him if he'd like to see some women undressing, an offer he declined because, as he explained, as a film producer he regularly saw too much of that sort of thing.

He ate a solitary meal in the dining-room and then, with a gradually descending heart, he went out into the myriad streets of London and walked among the lights and the faces. Everybody was full of Christmas joy, pushing along the pavements with parcels and girls. He saw his reflection in the window of a great store and thought how, with all that illumination and activity going on behind and around him, he looked so alone, like a watchman or a lost star.

The popularity of Charles W. Ricks was rapidly waning when he was rescued and transformed by his chance meeting with a girl he would never forget – Cecily-Ann Beauchamp, an international fashion designer from Worksop.

She had a settled plain face, but her skin was calm, her eyes untroubled from the frantic life she so obviously led in the *haute couture* salons of the world. 'I had to get away,' she told Caradoc just after he had introduced himself in the lounge of the hotel. She had been sitting alone reading a newspaper, and in an instant of inspired desperation he had approached and enquired whether the journal might by any chance be the *South Wales Echo*. It was not; in fact it proved to be *Racing Pigeon World*, which she had idly picked from the chair. But it was enough to produce a smile and a handshake. As a famous fashion designer she was more than delighted to meet an illustrious film producer, the only wonder being that they had not met before in some high-society party in some city of their wide worlds.

'Unfortunately,' said Cecily-Ann, 'I now realise that Christmas by yourself is not really Christmas, is it, lad?'

Caradoc liked and admired the way she had kept to her Midland accent despite her glamorous life. He must never let her discover he worked in the Pontycan gasworks. 'The same thing was just dawning on me,' he agreed. 'I suppose, in the end, it's a time to be with somebody.'

All at once he could not think of a single word to add. Nor, patently, could she. They faced each other awkwardly, her sitting, Caradoc standing, his hands moving about on their own like a pair of slow bats. It might have ended there, as so many promising things do end. From lack of conversation. Realising he might lose her to a silence at any moment, he blurted out the first thing that came to his tongue. 'Would you like to go to the zoo?' he asked.

She laughed aloud with surprise and relief. 'The zoo?' she repeated, her eyes meeting him half-way. 'Of course I would. But . . . but won't they be closed now?'

'Oh, yes. Yes, they're probably closed, at night. But tomorrow. I meant tomorrow, see.'

'Do they open zoos on Christmas Day?'

'I forgot about Christmas Day,' admitted Caradoc.

Cecily-Ann rose, and Caradoc saw how nice and thin she was. 'We could still go,' she suggested. 'We could look through the bars and wish the animals a merry Christmas.'

'Yes, that's the idea.' He hardly dared to speak for too long in case she got bored and went back to Worksop.

'I know,' she said with hushed excitement. 'Tomorrow, Christmas Day, let's do things that *nobody else will be doing*. Everybody will be indoors eating and drinking and sitting by their fires. Why don't we do a tour of London on our own?'

Caradoc could never remember being so suddenly pleased. Not even when Jones the Explosion was officially exonerated. 'That's a smashing idea,' he said. 'We'd have the whole place to ourselves.'

'Right, lad,' she said suddenly, holding out a hand that was so small it could only have belonged to a fashion designer. 'Tomorrow, then. I'll see you at breakfast, at eight o'clock, and we'll begin then.'

'You're going now?' asked Caradoc, a little disappointed.

'I have some dresses to design,' she shrugged. 'And then I shall go to sleep and dream about tomorrow.' She looked at him a little sharply. 'And what will you do, Charles?' she enquired.

Taken aback by the question, not to mention her calling

him Charles, whom he had almost forgotten in his new excitement, Caradoc stumbled, 'Oh, me, well, I'll be going to bed as well, I suppose. Retiring, that is. I have my new film to think about.'

'That's smashing,' she said in her uncompromising Worksop way. 'What is it going to be about?'

Again Caradoc panicked and said the first thing that came to his tongue. 'It's . . . oh, it's a musical version of the *Messiah*.'

There was a Christmasy mist dangling a few inches above the surface of the Regent Canal as they walked towards the zoo the next day. 'Like icing,' Cecily-Ann said.

'I thought the *Messiah* was musical already,' she said as they made their way below the softly dripping trees. They could have been walking alone in the world.

'The *Messiah*?' said Caradoc, once more disconcerted. 'Oh, it is. But this will be different. Dancing as well, see.'

'I suppose you meet a lot of young ladies in the film business,' she suggested cautiously. 'Dancers and that sort of lady.'

Caradoc sniffed. The air was so still and chill that he thought he felt it swirl around him with the sniff. 'Sometimes,' he answered. He was not anxious to be drawn into the subject of films. She was likewise modest about her triumphs in her world of models, designs and glamour. 'I'm not talking about frocks,' she had told him firmly as they set out. 'It's Christmas.'

They reached the railings of the zoo, glistening like the hanging crystals on a chandelier. When they got to the gate they saw that it was shut and locked, and they debated whether this might be to stop the people getting in or the inhabitants getting out. Carefully they patrolled along the railings again. 'Listen,' said Cecily-Ann with sudden excitement. 'I can hear them moving about inside.'

They put their ears near to the fence, turning their faces towards each other so that they were quite close. Caradoc looked at her carefully, but her eyes were shut as she listened so she did not look back. 'You're right,' he agreed. 'Moving they are. Might be a lion or a polar bear.'

Opening her eyes, she pushed her slim hands through the railings and tried to part the evergreen hedge. Caradoc gently took her fingers away and pushed in his own hands, used to turning bolts and screws at the gasworks. He parted the hedge sufficiently to see the face of a small bewildered ape looking back at him. 'Merry Christmas,' said Caradoc.

Cecily-Ann looked in through the foliage and shouted with surprise, but was then abruptly sad. 'He doesn't seem very happy, does he, Charlie?' she said. It was the first time she had called Caradoc Charlie.

'Very serious things, apes,' he said uncertainly.

'You've had experience with them in films, I suppose,' she said. They were walking along the echoing pavement again.

'In Madagascar,' said Caradoc, deciding not to open up any unexplored avenues. He had already told her about Madagascar.

'Yes, I suppose you would there,' she said. 'Can we go to see the River Thames?'

The question surprised and confused him. He did not know in which direction the River Thames lay.

'You shall,' he said decisively and, taking her arm, began to walk. It was a wondrous walk for two strangers. They went slowly, arms linked familiarly now, along the speechless avenues and terraces, only the Christmas breeze accompanying them. Occasionally a dog or a cat appeared but vanished quickly into some basement or alley. Buildings were shut and hushed, except for the big houses of the town people, which had lights and fairies in the windows and rings of holly at the door. But these houses were so massive that no festive noise leaked from them into the deserted streets. Not so much as a toot of a toy trumpet.

They walked then along the streets of stores, the windows looking back at them in blank surprise, the Yuletide displays abandoned without a second thought by customers and crowds. Cecily-Ann pointed at fashions in some of the stores, and Caradoc was surprised to find her so excited at seeing what for her must have been every-day things. The shuttered cinemas in the West End next claimed their attention, and they stood in the street while she encouraged him to point out the names of the famous stars he knew as his everyday working compan-ions.

They found themselves in the business streets; two figures in the cold and deserted canyons of the offices, walking almost gingerly, looking up at small remote windows, high, next to the roofs and the sky, where caretakers and their families were having their Christmases.

'Imagine them up there,' said Caradoc, pointing at one of the high squares of yellow. 'Getting ready for the Christmas dinner like people in a lighthouse.'

She smiled at the illusion, then together they looked at each other in alarm, near-panic.

'*Christmas dinner!*' exclaimed Caradoc. 'We mustn't miss Christmas dinner!'

'We've been having such a good time we forgot,' she whispered.

He caught her arm and they began to run along the pavements, around corners, down streets and through alleys. They were both laughing and gasping when, abrupt-ly, they turned a railinged corner and there, smiling at them benign and comforting, was the Regent Hotel.

Caradoc often remarked afterwards that Christmas din-ner that day was the best he had ever eaten (although, naturally, he never said that to his mam). They sat at a very posh little table in the window of the hotel. Outside the lace curtains the grey aged day drifted by with scarcely a move-ment. Cecily-Ann's plain face was as lively as a child's. Caradoc felt that he had known her for all the Christmases he could remember.

'I would have liked to buy you a present,' he said as sincerely as he could through a mouthful of plum pudding.

She looked up a little shocked. 'Oh, no, Charles!' she said. 'That would have *spoiled* it. The best thing is that we didn't have presents. The shops were closed. This day is a present for us both.'

It was a lovely speech and it touched his heart. He felt suddenly dishonest that he had told her all the fantasy about Charles W. Ricks, film producer. He began to dislike Charles W. Ricks even more. He would have liked to have heard her call him by his real name. Just once. But he was afraid she might be angry at the fraud, and she solved the matter – for a moment, anyway – by announcing that she was full of Christmas dinner and that she definitely wanted to see the River Thames, which had somehow escaped her attention during her frequent society forays to London. Caradoc stood up and wiped the crumbs of pudding from his lips. He would let the deceit go on a little longer.

The afternoon was dun-coloured, sleepy. It hardly raised an eyebrow as they went again walking through empty London. Pigeons pointed them out to each other in Trafalgar Square where the Christmas tree was shining but solitary. But eventually they reached it, just by the Houses of Parliament, with Big Ben's moon face beaming and the river moving like an old man going home. There was no movement anywhere in the earth or sky, as far as they could see. Not a bird. They stood on the very paunch of Westminster Bridge, two small figures in a great still Christmas-afternoon city.

Caradoc felt a sadness come over him as they stood looking, first up-river and then, running across the empty road, down the other way to where the Thames finally threaded its way into a hole in the London landscape. He knew that Cecily-Ann felt it, too. 'I don't think there will ever be another day like this, Charles,' she said simply.

They walked all the way back to the hotel. That evening in the dining-room they were quiet.

'I must go tomorrow,' she said. 'I have an important fashion show in Paris and I've got to get ready for it.'

'And I've got a lot of things to do as well,' nodded Caradoc understandingly. 'Next week I'm sailing for Hollywood.' He was not at all sure you *could* sail for Hollywood.

In their tabled silence he was all but overcome by the urge to tell her the truth, to pour out the story of how he had won the money, to tell her about his mam and Jones the Explosion and his world at far, far Pontycan. But she forestalled him by abruptly rising and saying sadly that it was time she went to bed.

He went as far as her door and there, for the first and last time, they exchanged a kiss. She went quickly into the room.

The next morning when Caradoc tried to find her she had already left the hotel. The porter said he had called a cab to take her to Euston.

Suddenly, blindly, Caradoc rushed from the hotel and vaulted into a taxi waiting outside. 'Euston!' he cried. 'And quick. It's a matter of life or death.'

Well, the driver had heard that before and there's no denying that he tried, but the long and short of it was that when Caradoc got to the gates of the platform the train was pulling out. Looking forlornly out of a retreating window was Mary Brown, a haberdasher's assistant of Worksop who, widowed after a glad year of marriage, had just spent the insurance money on that wonderful Christmas in London. As she looked from the train she saw him pounding along the platform. She knew he would never catch her. 'It's *Caradoc!*' he was shouting. 'I love you.'

'I'm Mary,' she shouted back. 'I love you, too.'

They called other things, addresses and the like, but it was all lost in the noise. The train and Cecily-Ann went away for ever and – who knows? – perhaps it was best that way.

Caradoc went back to Pontycan (much to his mam's relief, because she had not seriously expected to see him again and, in fact, was contemplating selling his bed), to the gasworks and Jones the Explosion.

He thought about her often and he could imagine her thinking about him. But he never saw her mentioned as a fashion designer in any newspapers and he did not go to London again for years, and then it was to Twickenham. He never had money like that again, either. It's not every day you win a hundred pounds on the football pools – a lot of money in 1935.